Letters from the Sea

by

Students of
La Quinta High School

La Quinta High School
Westminster, California

Letters from the Sea

Edited and Compiled by: Amanda LaPera
Copy Editors: Bryce Le, Brian Ly
Senior Section Editor: Diane Bui
Section Editors: Diane Bui, Keanu Hua, An Huynh, Colleen King, Michelle Lam, Shannon Le, Christine Vu, Kathleen Vu
Cover Designer: Vivien Nguyen
Interior Designer: Mariana Escalona Diaz

Published by La Quinta High School Creative Writing Class

Dedicated to the Class of 2020, With Love

Editor Preface

This year our world has experienced, and continues to endure, a historic pandemic. Covid-19 has sadly resulted in, as of the date of this publication, over 4.4 million people infected worldwide and the loss of over 300,000 lives, each one with their own story.

The publication of this book is a testament to the passion and perseverance of the creative spirit. Despite the suspension of in-person classes on Friday, March 13, the resulting technical difficulties, the challenges of arranging online author/editor meetings through Zoom, the stress of balancing online school, Covid-19 stay-at-home orders, and financial difficulties tied to the enormous unemployment rate, communication challenges and countless late nights, the editing team proclaimed the annual anthology publication must go on as planned.

With unwavering determination, scheduling meetings at odd hours, navigating the new but unprecedented educational reality, and fending off the mental health stress of isolation, our editing team nonetheless resolved that we only include the best of the student submissions to create a product everyone would be proud to publish and even more so in the midst of this chaos.

This book is the result of the hard work and dedication of the student authors and the Creative Writing editing team at La Quinta High School in Westminster, California.

—Amanda LaPera

QUARANTINE

by Michelle Rose

Snippets of news interlaced
Into formless days
Amorphous hours slide by
Follow my vacant gaze
Out picture windows
Framing a foreground view
Everything collapses inward
As isolation reigns
Like the queen of an island nation
Sometimes two souls, sometimes three, maybe five
But never more, no exceptions
Life contracts
Like the fading screen after a silent film
So quiet, so dark
Ripples moving towards each other
Progressively smaller until they disappear
Become nothing
The movements of life arrested

TABLE OF CONTENTS

It's a Desperate Feeling

by Ann Quach

Sonder, I'd like to know—of a life so far away—
of a person unknown—one passing glimpse of a day—
of memories I don't see and secrets I can't hear
the stories and the jokes, the joys and the fears—
the beginnings and the ends and everything in between
I'll peek—through the windows—at a world not mine to see.

Sonder, let me ask—of eloquent dramatics—
the stranger on the bus—the one in the back,
The passerby standing still on a crowded street,
a child laughing loud, smiling shyly at his feet
and the other who sits alone, big book in small hands—
With an existence like my own—just as boring and as grand.

Sonder, tell me, please—of all the truths and all the lies—
the meaningless thoughts of a life so simply alive.
I think it's the loneliness speaking—a feeling of travesty—
That on this planet of 7 billion people, in the sorrow of honest
reality,
we're all just faceless extras—transparent connections of chance—
passing windows—always wondering—without a second glance.

—It's a desperate feeling

OCEANS

by Diane Bui

Pacific,
Peaceful sister,
I pray that you grant me safe passage
As I journey across your vast territory.
Like you, I travel to meet my family,
To make connections between our
Distant selves despite the seldom visits.

Atlantic,
Mysterious sister,
We have only met on occasion,
But I wish you well all the same.
I have many questions, but you
Prefer the guessing game.
Or so I've heard from The Triangle.

Indian,
Dearest sister,
I hope your people treat you well
With the tributes and festivals that you
So much deserve for granting commerce,
Making so much travel possible
Between sovereign states.

Southern,
Youngest sister,
I didn't expect you here,
I thought you'd be at home
With the penguins you hold so dear.
Oftentimes you keep to yourself
You're so far away and yet so near.

Arctic,
Littlest sister,
How are you feeling?
Not too well it seems.
I send my goodwill,
and hopefully so will *they*.
I hope you fare well.

Sleep tight, kind oceans, you will be loved soon.

I AM A SECOND-GENERATION IMMIGRANT

by Ann Quach

My father tells me he wanted to be a doctor.
The bitter tang of lost dreams terrifies me.
When I take my APs, SATs, ACTs, they ask me
the highest level of education my parents have,
and when I bubble *some high school, some college,*
the sorrow smears from the hard-press of graphite onto paper.

I heard it takes three generations for a culture to assimilate.
Driving through *Little Saigon, USA,*
I see a community digging its heels into the dirt,
desperate to keep its roots.
My mother tells me they are stubborn people,
living in a faded past, they refuse to move forward.

Sometimes I feel as if she does not want to be Vietnamese,
as if she would rather shed her heritage like snakeskin
to become a perfect American.

But I see the boar's tooth she carries on her keychain
and I remember the tragedies she lives with—
a father and brother lost at sea, a family left behind.
She tells me she is alone here—without her brothers and
sisters—
I want to tell her she has me,
but that type of hurt bore a hole in her heart long before my birth
and there is nothing my American Band-Aids can do.

My father returned to his homeland
for the first time in fifteen years last summer—
but when I asked if he was happy,
he told me in quiet words, *It is not the Vietnam I know.*
I think a piece of my heart broke along with his.
I see his tired eyes and worn hands—
he has worked all his life—
overflowing vacation days left unused—

and when I ask him, *What for?*
he tells me, *For you.*
Always, for you.

—I am a second-generation immigrant

DREAM CHASER

by Benson Truong

By definition, a dream is a series of visions that occur involuntarily during sleep.
Experts cannot fully grasp this concept, far too complicated and deep.
Sometimes creative and light-hearted as talking sheep.
Or worse, taking a mysterious, life-threatening leap.
But, words cannot convey what dreams expose.
That's why I have a theory that I want to propose.
Scientists hypothesized these sensations are what our subconscious mind has composed
But I'm here to say that these fantasies are real, a parallel world, I suppose.
When it's day for you, it's night to them,
When it's night for you, it's day to them.
And when you fall into your slumber, you'll be on that spectrum.
You dream of visiting places you haven't been to before.
Because those are the places that they have explored.
You have dreamt of peculiar events.
Because those events have yet to commence.
Sometimes it's so realistic,
You'd wake up and ponder, "Was I a part of it?"
Ever heard of lucid dreaming?
The act of controlling "yourself" within that world.
It takes time to master, but once you do,
You get to play with a brand new you.
But what's stopping them from lucid dreaming, too?
What if your reality is their domain to play?
All of your relationships, something they create.
Everything in your life is false.
In other words, it's all a paradox.

NOT TODAY

by Benson Truong

I'm not ready to go.
I know I can be stronger,
but I can't survive any longer.
Blood and sweat run down my body,
dragging me to the ground.
Like sand in an hourglass,
it drains rapidly.
My confidence flows from me.
I'm not ready to go.
Broken and battered,
I attempt to stand.
I fall and sink,
as if caught in quicksand.
I sit isolated from all,
I'm blocked by a wall.
I try to change my path,
I end up getting lost.
I'm not ready to go.
But I guess this is the end.
Until,

you reach out, lifting up my spirits,
refueling me with energy and might,
giving me another reason to fight.
I'm not alone,
I can't do this on my own.
I shouldn't rely on myself,
I have friends.
I have family.
No, it won't end today.
I won't die today.

MY DEAR AUNT

by Michelle Lam

Her hands were cold
Bony and thin and rustic gold
And her eyes were large and round
Reflecting the room in dark brown
And in that reflection was me
As I watched her wither, helplessly
But that wasn't what she left behind
For even now in my mind
She is a dancing laughing flower
Her face pink with fresh powder
Dark hair curled into her forehead
Like petals to the pistil in a flowerbed
Arms outstretched in the sun
Holding orchid branches in one
With the sweet promise to me
That she is in my garden, free

With love,
Your Niece

FROM DEVIL TO HUMAN

by Kenneth Tran

"IT SADDENS ME TO know that I had the greatest hand in your design. You were built to be incomparable, but destiny unfortunately laid you out on the worst path conceivable. In your heart and soul rests an endless well of hatred and jealousy. It cannot exist here. You cannot exist here." These final words branded into him, giving the Devil something to replace the divine wings he lost.

A truly repulsive creature he is, and he knows it. There is no reprieve in his looks. Everywhere, he is hideous. Every inch of his skin, dried and peeled like the shedding of a snake. His eyes and mouth—the darkest specks of a void. His hair—tangled webs that dangle to the ground. Rags that hang threadbare.

Who did this to him? You know who.

You pray to him every day. Look at him like he's the greatest creation of his own omnipotence. But if you were to take one look at this creature, you would know who the real devil is.

He, who is a cursed animal, cannot do the normal things one would take for granted. Like Tantalus, he is rejected the luxury of water and food. And unlike Narcissus, he cannot see himself even before mirrors of the highest quality. But these curses pale in comparison to the one thing that truly keeps him grounded as the "Devil." Any living thing that gets near him, with or without his consent, dies.

These qualities that now define him were placed for breaking his father's most sacred rules. They ruined him, wore down his once celestial body and, most notably, his once cold heart. See, the more he killed, the more he became in love with life. The more he killed, the more he suffered.

He couldn't stand living on earth, eternally destroying the final thing that kept him sane. His brothers and sisters had visited him frequently in the beginning, but at some point, they stopped altogether. He had no one. He was destined to be alone.

He secluded himself in a place called the Underworld. Here the rocks protrude from every wall like rows of teeth, while eyeless creatures lurk in the shadowy mist. And here he has stayed for several millennia, doing nothing other than reflect. He would be safe here—safe from the millions of discriminating eyes. But most of all, he would be safe from himself, his own destructive power.

Countless years passed before he finally saw another living person. A girl, around six years of age, had appeared before his sight. They were only separated by a small stream of fire. His body shivered in excitement, and then he remembered all the people he had killed with his curse. Their horrified faces materialized in his mind and refused to leave.

Turn around, he told himself. But he couldn't. His nervous eyes shifted around until it made contact with hers. He saw her face lift up in happiness. Of course she was happy. He had spent thousands of years here without seeing anything resembling a human. That meant the same was true for her. How long was she here, all alone?

Unable to contain her emotions, she ran towards him, using the small rocks scattered on the surface of the stream of fire to close the distance. But the heat was intense; she hesitated her jump halfway in. The girl wasn't going to make it.

Without thinking, he shifted to the shadows next to her, grabbed her arm, and moved her to safety. In an instant her body started crumbling into dust. He let go just as he realized, but it was too late. The faces in his mind distorted into horrific creatures and started invading his ears with yells.

"Monster!"

That's right. That's what I am.

He closed his eyes and lightly scrunched his face. He was ready for them, those piercing screams and fearful looks. But nothing ever came. He peeked out from the comfort of his own eyelids. She was looking at him, eyes gleaming in astonishment and curiosity. She smiled.

"Thank you, sir." Last he heard the wind's whisper as it carried her away in pieces.

The Devil's body was frozen still, but an earthquake rumbled inside his head. He had been scorned and neglected in God's world for his entire existence. In the countless eons he never dreamed he could be worthy of anything, let alone gratitude. Yet a little human, with every reason to hate the face of sin for killing her, saw in it a worth that the Devil himself had never seen.

Enough.

He tilted his head back and peered into the sky.

Enough.

For the first time, his body felt light. He felt free.

Enough.

Humanity's innocence had moved him. Humans do wrong, and yet they are still redeemable. Forgiveness is what defines the race. It's how they progress, how they live. He now knew what he had to do. He had to ask his father to unshackle him. He needed to show his father what that little girl taught him—something he has always wanted deep down.

"Let me be human."

IRON AND ICHOR

by Kayla Nguyen

The world ended yesterday.
The sea foamed blood
And cried candy red rivers
That rained judgment on us from the heavens.

The sky swam alongside stardust whales,
And schools of dead fish took to the skies
While the clouds were clogged with pearls.
Chaos couldn't be more beautiful.

We watched
As the moon was drenched in red,
As the atmosphere closed in on us,
As the stars were slaughtered, one by one.

Seeing your moonlit profile
Should have been a catharsis,
Or perhaps a sign of forgiveness
For someone as unholy as me.

My mouth was crawling with tension
Drier than the magma-crusted earth.
The gentle rise and fall of your chest
Lured me into asking a doomed question:

Would you go with me?
The words came out in a rush of flames.
Would you go with me
To the end?

Your dark, melancholic eyes shuddered
And looked away.
Then you said the exact word I was dreading:
No.

I couldn't fathom how our fantasy
Could fall apart so easily with a simple word.
Our mournful minds and strawberry-flavored summers
All vanished in the wake of something greater.

You used to say my name like a delicate prayer
And we used to love so sweet,
So warm, and not so different
From how the dead yearn for sleep.

Every time I heard you call for me
In the dead of night,
Or the wake of spring mornings,
I wanted to knit our heartbeats together.

I threw myself into your depths,
Your velvet singularities and honeyed multitudes,
The soft fiber of who you are,
Only to have it slip out of my grasp.

I stared at the red string of fate
stringing us together, then back at you.
I did the only sensible thing I could do:
I walked away.

I walked away from the only person
I stayed for,
And told myself
I didn't feel a single thing.

We were two halves
Of one celestial whole,
But both of us shattered
Under the weight of words.

Our world ended today.
It ended in an explosion
Of ash and fury and starlight
That ruined us beyond infinity.

The sea was still gurgling iron
And the sky was still dipping its light toes
In the delicate destruction eating away at it.
The chaos was still beautiful.

I watched
the show of sparks, the primordial bath
Breathing life into itself
Through seas of ambrosia and death.

I saw your moonlit profile
Lying parallel to my own
But perpendicular to a path of ruin.
Your face was frozen in time.

My throat was scarlet and raw
From screams stuttering through the smoky heat,
But my voice yearned to linger on yours
In futile calls of your name.

You don't respond.
Our teeth and souls are stained with death;
You bleed iron in the guise of honey,
And I bleed ichor right beside you.

We lie there, bleeding love and loss
At the dusk of the end of the world
And in the darkness of our wasted Earth
As we await divine punishment.

Was it worth it?
The almighty, blind, all-seeing creator asked.
World eater, was the shining red dawn
Deserving of the void dusk?

Is your world deserving of this fate?
World eater, is the salted earth meant to burn,
Or is it meant to quench your spirit?
World eater, would you still fall, even after all this time?

I said, *Lord,*
I am doing what fate has commanded me to.
Do you think that I did not wish to fall?
Do you think that I wished to live in your imperfect utopia?

Lord, I am where you cast me to be;
I have shed my glass canines and gunmetal bones
For a life worth living, but I tell myself
The world ended for a good cause.

Lord, let it be known
That no matter how much I long for his touch,
He can never be soft nor mine, so we are never to reunite.
The world ended,

And it was for love.
I did it for love.
I did it to save him;
Nothing more, nothing less.

THE WISE MAN AND THE FOOL

by Kimbill Ly

A wise man once told me
What I would grow up to be
A "Prodigy," he gleamed, whole-heartedly
In my naive adolescence, I believed his words
Blinded by pride, deafened by lies,
His promise eased my mind
I trusted his prophecy,
Not knowing that this mistake would end in tragedy
He disappeared soon after,
Leaving me to wait like a dog for his master
I waited and waited and waited some more,
Never once doubting his fore-told lore
When adulthood finally arrived,
He returned to me undisguised,
Unsurprised that my success did not materialize
He laughed and mocked me in front of my eyes,
Finally acknowledging his pathetic lie
I questioned the wise man, asking him why
Why he would trick me and humiliate me so heartlessly
Why he would revel in my sorrow and abuse my trust
Why he would call himself a "wise man" if he had no sense of just
It was then that I realized the truth behind the "wise man"
He did not become a "wise man" from wisdom and dignity
He became a "wise man" from deceit and trickery
The "wise man" only needed a puppet,
A fool to be duped and corrupted
I was ashamed and regretful, as I had become his tool
I was the duped one, I was the Fool

TRUTH

by Kimbill Ly

The Truth is, none of it matters
None of it, not the gossip nor the chatter
Whether we like it or not,
Our lives will become lost
And what we say won't matter
Before we know it, we'll vanish into thin air
And we'll finally realize that life isn't so rare
And through our journey to the end,
We'll learn to gather up our family and friends
And as we drift into an eternal slumber
We know that together, we'll rest forever
The Truth is, none of it matters
But that doesn't mean you should mope and get sadder
Our lives will fade over time,
But our memories will remain in their prime

SLEEPING CITIES

by Diane Bui

Citizens fall fast asleep,
Powder fills their noses and lungs,
A pleasant aroma worms its way inside.

Men slumber on earth,
Shiny trinkets beside them,
Waiting for them to play catch again.

Women at home,
Cheerfully await their men's return,
So they can cook on their patient stoves.

Children play outside,
Throwing rubber balls at each other,
With a hit, they laugh and lie on the ground,
"Out," they call.

Elsewhere,
People dance and cheer while soldiers
March off in parades donning
Crimson uniforms with silver accents.

Buildings bow to prominent generals,
Shadows cower to the light,
Darkness returns to its hiding place.

Back at home,
Men, women, and children,
Laugh, dance, and sing,
And another man dies.

NIGHT

by Diane Bui

Look through the glass
What do you see?
"Only stars and things."
Well, the night sky smiles tonight,
Starry freckles twinkle against dark complexion.
She is adorned by Sagittarius,
Bow in hand, quiver strapped to her back,
Arrow notched and aimed West.
Her gown shimmers with celestial sequins.
Blue, indigo, violet, pink—meld into her skirt.
She wears Venus and Mars on her ears.
Her pendant, shining Luna,
Rains love upon us tonight.
She's here for only a few more hours
Before her brother wakes.
What do you have to say to her now?

MOTHER

by Alexa Wright

08/19/06

I HATE MY JOB. I hate my life. And I hate the caws of those stupid crows. I hate waking up at five every morning. I hate wasting my precious life slaving away at a minimum wage job. I hate the insincere smiles, and I sure as hell hate the condescending voice of my whale of a manager.

God, how did I get here? What happened to that hope and unwavering optimism? What happened to that bright young man from thirty years ago?

He's dead. The world killed him—murdered him without a thought of what could've been. If anything, this is all my fault. It's practically the world's job to crush the life out of us all, yet my innocence blinded me to this truth. I was woefully unprepared, and the world took advantage of me.

Bwah, look at all this disgusting philosophical dribble. I can't believe Dr. Boes got me to buy into his dumb diary idea. I still can't believe he gets paid to sit around all day and ask dumb questions. Thank god he's covered by my insurance. I'd rather set a stack of twenties on fire than give that lazy slob my money.

But I've got to hand it to him—he sure knows how to game the system. If I could get paid to do nothing, I sure as hell would. I guess I can't blame him for being clever.

His diary idea is still full of junk though. I don't see how any of this is supposed to help me. If anything, this diary is reminding me of specifically why I dread my existence.

Dr. Boes, if you are reading this, you should seriously consider getting a new job. Also, it wouldn't kill you to shower every once in a while. You don't live in a barn, and you aren't a horse, so stop bathing like one.

08/25/06

It's my lucky day. A kid threw up in the restaurant's playground. I swear, that little demon intentionally chose the most cramped place to regurgitate his lunch. I hope that kid grows up to be just like me. I hope with all my heart he gets paid barely anything to experience the joy that is cleaning vomit and boogers.

Ron, my manager, always gives me the worst tasks. Yesterday, it was cleaning the garbage disposal, today it was cleaning vomit, and I bet tomorrow it will be filing the restaurant's tax returns. I can't tell if he's trying to make me quit or if he delights in my suffering. I wouldn't be surprised if he had sadistic tendencies. After all, it takes a very *special* person to want to run a place full of miserable employees and screaming children.

But I guess that's just Ron.

I spent the rest of the day flipping burger patties. While certainly a better alternative to cleaning vomit, patty flipping is mind-numbingly boring. Even a zombie could do it. At one point, I tried to see if I could hit a fly with a perfect patty flip. I was having a great time until my coworker spotted the fly and smacked it with a bug swatter. I spent the rest of the day in a catatonic state, only occasionally lifting my arm to flip a burning patty.

Thanks Barbara, you're a real doll.

09/02/06

It's the twentieth anniversary of my mother's death. I asked Ron if I could take the day off to commemorate her, and he said yes. I guess he does have a heart after all.

I spent the day listening to her favorite music and remembering all the times she took me out to eat ice cream. It's so long ago, but still feels like yesterday. It was yesterday when she forgot who I was—yesterday when I saw her shriveled husk lying on her deathbed.

Dementia is a cruel mistress. She taints the sanctity of the human mind—she steals the one thing that makes each of us unique. It's not enough to kill us. No, she has to make us suffer—she has to force everyone to watch the deterioration of their loved ones.

But my mother's dementia wasn't just the run of the mill evil. No—her dementia was a special type of wicked. Long before she lost herself, she was a miserable mess of unwavering anxiety. She never looked happy, and swore on her life that someone was after her. I couldn't stand seeing her so terrified. I put her in a home, something I still regret to this day.

By the time she passed, my mother wasn't the woman who took care of me for so many years. She was just a body: a fleshy automata with no memories, no hopes, no dreams, no fears, no regrets. I hate that this is what I often remember her by. Not as the spunky woman with a heart of gold, but as an empty vessel festering in a hospital bed.

I miss you, Mom. I'm sorry for the person I've become. I'm sorry I gave up on you when you needed me the most. I'm sorry that I couldn't make you proud.

09/10/06

My last entry was quite a read, to say the least. It's so...unlike me. Well, at least I can always count on having a soul for at least one day per year.

On a separate note, I've been struggling to fall asleep for the past few days. I assumed this was probably because of all the coffee I'd been drinking, so I put down the bean water.

Not only am I still sleep deprived, but I also feel like the south end of a northbound donkey. I never noticed the extent of my caffeine dependency until now, and I can say with certainty that I do not have the desire to fix it any time soon.

Work was all right. It wasn't great, but at least nobody died in our bathroom today. I spent the day deep-frying the slices of decaying potato corpses. My coworkers hate how I describe french fries, but I hate the way all of them breathe through their mouths, so I guess we're even.

At the very least, making french fries isn't as soul crushing as patty flipping. There are a lot of unique potato shapes, and even more ways to slice them. The same can't be said for our frozen patties. They all look exactly the same, but I guarantee that they each have a unique mixture of toes, organs, and other mystery meats. I guess patties and fries aren't so different after all.

09/15/06

Sometimes, I wish I could run away from it all. I wish I could simply pack up all my bags, and set up a homestead in Nebraska. I could live off the land, grow my own food, hunt my own rabbits, and build my own cute windmill.

I don't know why I even bother to have dreams anymore. I'm just giving myself false hope and setting myself up for misery. I can't escape my life. Even if I could run off to Nebraska, nothing would change. I am the common denominator in all of this, and undoubtedly, there is something wrong with me. I don't think anything could help me change—not Dr. Boes, not this dumb journal, and not a fresh start.

09/24/06

Thank God for coffee. I don't think I'd be able to hold my job if it wasn't for that sweet, delectable bean water.

This past week has been absolute hell. Last night, I wasted five hours staring at my cheap alarm clock. I swear, that thing was mocking my suffering. The digital red numbers glared into my eyes, goading me into fixating all my attention on it. I snatched the damn thing and chucked it across the room.

I slept peacefully for the next four hours.

10/03/06

I'm such an idiot.

I fell asleep behind the wheel and rear-ended a parked car. A parked car. What kind of absolute clown hits a parked car? I'm becoming a real special kind of stupid, aren't I?

I had to drive off. I don't have any insurance, and I sure as hell don't have enough cash to cover the damages out of pocket. I don't think anyone saw me, but I don't know. There could've been someone looking out of an apartment window, or someone walking a dog, or a store security camera.

I hope not. My life would be over. I don't think I'd be able to pay the fines and fees, and I'd undoubtedly end up penniless on the street. I don't know what to do. Maybe if I get some rest, I'll have a clearer mind. Yeah, I'll know what to do.

10/15/06

The police haven't come for me yet. I think I may be safe. I still slept horribly last night, but that's fine. I took a different route to work. It ended up taking an hour to get there, but that's an hour I'm willing to sacrifice to keep my freedom.

My manager was awful today. He scolded me for dropping the potatoes, even though it wasn't me. I swear it felt like someone else was moving my arms and legs. When I mentioned this, he stomped his feet and told me to quit making excuses. Ron sucks.

Nothing else notable happened today, although I felt like I was being watched. I don't quite know how to explain it other than feeling someone's eyes watching me. I'm not sure if I should bring this up to Dr. Boes next time I see him...

10/20/06

I'm really beginning to worry that there is someone watching me. I know, I know, it sounds odd, but I swear, I can feel someone's eyes on me. It's like some sixth sense, or gut feeling, or something. I don't know if I should trust this feeling. I always hear people emphasizing the importance of trusting your instincts, but I really don't know if I can anymore. I think there is someone else in me, and I hope to God I don't lose myself.

I don't know what to do anymore. I don't know if I will be okay. I don't know if I can trust myself.

10/25/06

I found a microphone in my burger patty today. I was hungry while I was making patties, and I just needed a nibble. I don't know what it was doing there, but I suspect I'm being spied on.

This person is really good. I don't know how they got it there without me noticing nor how they knew I was going to eat that specific patty. I think I have an idea of who it could be, but I really hope my suspicions are wrong.

10/31/06

They're coming for me. They're coming to ruin my life and take everything I have. I know they're watching me. Someone must've seen me hit that car. The police have my plate numbers, and they're coming to take me to jail.

My co-workers don't believe me. They say I've lost it. But they're wrong—I'm not losing it, I committed a crime and now I'm going to be punished for it. This happens all the time. People break the law, and then the police come for them. If anything, my co-workers have lost it! How can they believe that the law wouldn't come for a criminal? I can't believe how naive they are.

11/10/06

My coworkers are in on it. They have to be. I've told them so much, yet they don't believe me. They have to be gas lighting me so I'll feel safe confiding in them. But they don't know that I know what they're doing. I know they're talking to the police, telling them all I've done so they can arrest me.

I'm not an idiot! I know they're scheming and planning. I can't believe they think I'm that stupid. How dare they do this to me? I thought we were fine together, but I guess they don't care about me losing everything.

11/25/06

I was right! I'm not losing it! The police came for me and took me into custody. I confronted Barbara today, and my manager called the police. They were all working with the police, just as I suspected.

I spoke with one of the officers and told him how all of my coworkers hate me and want to get me in trouble. He must've agreed, because he let me walk free. He must know about the truth. He must know the police are corrupt, and they're using people's friends to spy on them.

11/26/06

I guess I don't work at the restaurant anymore. I came in for work this morning and my manager threatened to call the police. Whatever, I hate that place. Why would I want to work at a place filled with government plants?

I had a strange dream last night. I was inside an enormous wasp, and I controlled it like a robot. Then the wasp stopped and spoke to me.

"You are rotting, my child."

Then I woke up. I haven't slept this well in so long. I miss the wasp.

12/08/06

I woke up this morning and my hand was gone. It didn't hurt, and I could still feel it, but it just wasn't there. I tried looking for it everywhere, but I couldn't find it. I checked my closet, my sink, and even the trash can, but there was nothing. Where could it have gone?

My coffee machine stopped working today. I don't know why, but it just stopped. I asked it why it stopped, but it didn't want to talk to me. I think I forgot to feed it.

12/17/06

I finally found my hand today! It was under my pillow! What a sneaky little bugger. I tried to grab it to reattach it to my arm, but it fell to the floor and scurried under the bed. He's really good at hiding. I can't remember how long it took for me to reattach him, but when he was finally back on my arm, the sun was gone. Maybe my hand is afraid of the moon.

I dreamt about the wasp again, but she stopped talking to me. She only screams now. I wonder what she's afraid of. I asked her why, but she only screamed louder.

I don't like her anymore.

1/111/07

Today is one day. I think one is a very interesting number. It's so pointy and proud, and I wish I could be just like it.

My coffee machine isn't eating. I put a burger in his pot a week ago, and the burger is still there. Now he smells awful, and I'm not sure if I should bring him to the vet. I hope he doesn't have sepsis.

2/0/07

I lost my journal, but I found it now. It crawled away from me in my sleep and hid in the shower. I decided to tape it to my body so it can't run away from me.

Today my landlord knocked on my door. He said there was a complaint about a smell. I don't know what he's talking about. I told him to leave me alone, and he did. But before he left, he gave me a piece of paper that said *eviction notice*. That word sounds familiar, but I can't quite remember what it means. Maybe I can get some sleep and I'll figure it out.

e/7/03

I found out what eviction means. It means people get to steal your house. That's such a dumb word, I don't know why they bothered to invent it.

But, now I have a new home. I live with a man named Hank. He smells a bit, but he lets me stay in his alley. He's a cool guy.

1/5/06

I went to go pick some flowers for a soup, but I found a lake instead. I went for a swim, and it was a very nice feeling. A lady yelled at me to get out of the water, but she's not yelling anymore. I didn't find flowers, but I found a pretty rock.

Hank keeps yelling at me to stop being so noisy at night. It's not my fault I can't sleep. I try and try to close my eyes but then the Smiling Man comes. He likes to visit when I try to sleep. His mouth is so long. I think that's how he's able to fit so many teeth inside. His gross face scares me, it's like a rotting pear that's gray and fleshy. I want him to go away. Maybe if he's gone, I can sleep, even just a little.

07/77/07/07

Hank won't talk to me anymore. I don't know what I did. I think he's mad at me. He smells really bad today too. I think he forgot to shower. Maybe he's not mad at me. Maybe he's just embarrassed.

I see the Smiling Man more. Even when my eyes are open, he's here. He likes to sit behind me. His breath smells like Hank, and it feels sticky. But I'm not scared of him anymore. He said he needs me. He says that Mother needs me. I don't know what he means, but I want to see my mom. I miss her a lot. I want to get ice cream with her again.

04/A

The Smiling Man told me he needs Hank's body. He said Hank is on vacation and he isn't using it anymore. I said that Hank isn't on vacation, he's right here. The Smiling Man just looked at me and laughed. He looks gross when he laughs, like an old clam with teeth. I don't understand what is so funny.

He says that Mother's children need a home, but I don't understand what he means. I already have a home with Hank. My home isn't nice, but it's a home.

He left and took Hank. I'm glad it doesn't smell anymore, but I miss Hank. Hank tells the funniest jokes.

08/

The Smiling Man came back with breakfast. I was really hungry all night. I'm glad he's my friend. He gave me stew. He said it was a gift from Mother.

I don't remember Mom being such a bad cook. The stew was gross. I don't think she cooked it long enough. I lied to the Smiling Man. I said it was delicious. I didn't want to hurt Mom's feelings.

The Smiling Man says I'll get to meet Mother soon. I'm so excited! I haven't seen her in so long. I want to tell her about Hank and the Smiling Man and everything.

I went to the store this morning. A pretty lady gave me a dollar. I bought chocolate. It was the best thing I ever tasted. I wish I had more chocolate. I came back to the alley, and it was covered in sticky red stuff.

The Smiling Man said that Mother didn't like the way the alley looked. I think it looks bad now, but I didn't say anything. It smells bad too. It smells like the time I put a magnet in my nose. I asked the Smiling Man why it smelled. He said this was how Mother wanted it to smell. She's stranger than I remember.

I still haven't seen Mom yet. I wonder when I can see her. The Smiling Man says soon, but I don't think he knows what soon means.

4

Mom looks different. I don't remember Mom being so big. But I don't remember a lot of things. Mom looks like a bug, but I can't remember what the bug was called.

Mom said that it is time. I didn't know what time it was, but I guess she did. Mom is so smart. I'm glad she's my mom.

But I don't know why Mom hurt me. She sliced my belly open and put orbs inside. Then she spat something gooey out and sewed my belly back together. The Smiling Man said that Mother loves me. He said that she hurt me because I'm her favorite. I'm so happy that Mom isn't mad at me, and I'm more happy that I'm her favorite. I gave Mom a hug, and she left.

/

I don't feel good. After Mom hurt me, my stomach hurts really bad. It's really big now, like a balloon. I asked the Smiling Man why my belly is so big. He said that it is because Mother loves me. Mother's children need a home.

I don't think I need to live in my stomach. I told the Smiling Man this, and he laughed. I don't know what was so funny. I don't think he's all right in the head. He's starting to scare me again.

My stomach is moving a lot. I thought it was the food I ate, but I haven't eaten anything in a long time. I asked the Smiling Man about it, but he wouldn't tell me why. He only stared at me. He gave me more stew. It was still gross, but I ate it. I love Mom, and I don't want her to be sad.

I keep having dreams. I don't know how. I don't sleep anymore. I dreamt about Mom. She flew over the city and she cut the ground. She gave the ground a face, just like the Smiling Man's face.

I asked the Smiling Man about this. He says the ground has a face to help give Mother's children a home. I told him I already have a home, but he looked at me funny.

Mom will visit soon. I don't know when she will, but it is soon. I can feel it. The Smiling Man is excited, too. He says that Mother will bring gifts. I wonder what kind of gifts.

The Smiling Man said we need to leave the alley. I like the alley. I don't want to leave. He said that Mother wants to meet us in a very special place.

Mom is here! She broke the sky and cut the ground. The Smiling Man was laughing. He cut my belly, and a bunch of bugs came out. I finally figured out why my stomach looked so weird.

The face in the ground started screaming louder than the people on the street. Everyone started to leak red from their eyes. They stopped moving. I think they're sleeping now.

Mother and the bugs are eating the eyes of the sleeping people. I don't know how they haven't woken up yet.

I don't think she's my mom.

I see the teeth in the sky. There were a lot of teeth, maybe even more than the Smiling Man. The sky was all red, too. The building's walls are warm and red and smell gross. The face is screaming very loud and eating all the buildings. I think the Smiling Man is laughing or screaming. I don't understand what's so funny.

It's very dark now. I'm starting to feel sleepy. I haven't slept in so long. I think this is Mom's gift. I think   S

              H   K

                   E

                          N   O

FEED ME CLOUDS

by Andrea Torres

Feed me clouds
So I don't have to taste anything.
I wish to eat soft nothingness and feel lightweight
As the feathers that cling to a bird,
Like a pillow of marshmallows.
A body that can feed off of puffiness and the color white.
That is what I most desire.
The coursing of moisture through my veins,
That cloud nesting inside my abdomen without harm.
My sky of a stomach will keep it company,
And nutrients of stars will come out when it is night time.

FRECKLES

by Andrea Torres

If my face were a canvas, it would be an imperfect one.
If it were to be colored, it would be a fair peach tone.
If there were to be shapes, there would be intricate circles and lines.
My canvas of a face, a gift bestowed upon me by the universe's will.
My eyelashes of midnight complement my oval eyes: jewels of hazel.
My lips of rose complement the peach fuzziness of my face moss.
Brown arches clothe my forehead like angel wings.
What makes this canvas so imperfect then?
It must be the splotches of sepia
Scattered across like droplets onto the masterpiece.
A stranger to normal beauty, yet provides gentleness to the structure.
A symbol demonstrating my innocence and youth.
If this is how God painted my face, I will gladly accept his work.
This face I own is unique:
No one can replicate these spots tainting the work of art.
My features are not yours to judge.
A perfect face does not exist.
My freckles are proof of that.

WHERE DO WE GO?

by Kayla Nguyen

Where do we go when we die?

"We go into the ground,"
A broken boy speaks out in the midst of adolescence.
"We just become bones and dust and dirt,
While everyone else continues their monotonous lives."

Empty promises dangle in the air
Like a fairytale curse.
The rusty swings creak and groan
Underneath the weight of pretty little lies.

"We're just piles of flesh and bone;
Forgotten and cold in the ground.
At least the dirt would check my petals for bruising."
He was always such a nihilist.

"I like to think that we go to a special place,"
A less fractured yet still dented girl replies.
Soft voice cracking as she speaks,
After her guilt becomes too heavy to bear.

She tilts her head up to the heavens,
And unshed tears of diamond glitter.
Silently, she mourns her past
And hopes for the future.

"I like to imagine that after we stop waking up,
We just appear in an oasis
Where everybody we love
Comes back to us."

"It'd be a place where we can finally rest,
A place where we can finally reunite with
Our lost moms, dads, sisters, and brothers.
I like to think that that's our heaven."

A dark-haired, apathetic boy
Stares into his devastatingly empty palms.
The lonely child within him wishes
They could finally be filled with a purpose.

"We don't go anywhere.
We stay here and wither away
Just to see everyone else live out
Their happily-ever-afters."

His hair is all tangles and curls from the breeze,
But he ignores it as bruises blossom
On invisible skin,
As the paper-thin façade wavers.

"We don't reincarnate,
Go to heaven,
Or chill in the underworld.
It's just an empty void."

The numbness of a black hole
That has inhaled all the stars in the sky
Eats away at the child-like wonder
He abandoned.

"Don't we go to the stars?"
A golden supernova of a girl whispers,
Not knowing that she herself
Was born a child of the cosmos.

"After death,
We aren't confined to
The laws of the living anymore.
We can go wherever we want."

Her sunflower hair illuminates the room,
And speckles of stardust pepper her porcelain features.
Her sunset eyes flicker to the night sky
She calls home.

"I want to go up there.
We belong to the stars.
After all, where else
Would we love to return?"

SPRING NIGHT

by Brian Ly

A youthful night for a youthful pair.
Spring air chilled our skin,
But the warmth of being together
Satisfied our needs.

You ran ahead in laughter,
And paused a few steps in front,
Hair waving in the wind,
Smile towards the amber horizon.

A simple sight, it was,
But one to remember, nonetheless.
We were alone in our own world,
You and I.

Even if only for a moment,
Time slowed to a halt.
You grabbed my attention,
Never letting go of it since.

When I told you how I felt,
When you turned back with teary eyes,
When the first chapter of our story began,
It all happened on that youthful Spring night.

THEY TOLD US

by Kayla Nguyen

When we were all young
And thriving in our gardens
Of ignorant bliss

When we were all bathing
In the ecstasy of the flowers we picked
And the laughter we shared

When we were all whispering
Under our blankets of the heavens
And running around in our makeshift capes
Made from unruly ocean waves,

They told us,
"Look both ways before crossing the street."

They told us,
"Never talk to strangers."

They told us,
"Never wear your heart on your sleeve."

Being in the prime of adolescence,
We never listened.

Our hearts remained stitched on our sleeves,
And our love continued to lie there, bleeding.

How else were we supposed
To feel the rolls of thunder
Roaring under our skin?

How else were we supposed to know
That the infinite cosmos
Lie within our very bones and fragile rib cages?

How else were we supposed to sense
The flowers that eternally bloom with abandonment
And wilt with the weight of words inside our hearts?

Our affinity and curiosity
To converse with the oddest of people never lessened.

After all,
How else was the world to know
We were still drowning in bottomless pools
Spiked with the loveliest of poisons?

How else were we going to know
That we never built homes
Out of our own hollow shells?

How else were we going to know
That our flaws could never be peeled off,
That we were trapped within ourselves?

Their words fell upon deaf ears, and alas,
We crossed the road without looking both ways.

HOME

by An Huynh

A person cannot
truly be homeless,
for there resides
a home in their heart.
A person can be houseless,
for many are
sleepers of the streets.
But to call the houseless
homeless is to say that
they have no place
to belong anymore.

Lost eyes wander aimlessly
with tired feet restless
on the cold pavement,
freezing and yearning
for a place to feel safe,
receiving looks
of pity and disgust.
But in their hearts
there is a memory of a home.

A reminder of the
love and affection
they had received
over the years.
A house of memories
Stamped
within the heart,
sheltering them from
the despair of loneliness,

helping them to survive
through the harsh nights.

And although they know
that these memories
alone won't
end their struggle,
they live on
with the hope that
someday,
they'll regain those
precious moments
of warmth

A LITTLE BIRD

by Keanu Hua

MOM AND DAD ARE kind of weird.

They always say they loved each other, with a *d*. That means past tense, but they're still married, and marriage means that you love someone a lot. So why argue so much? Watching TV or eating dinner by myself, I hear them yelling because we have a small house. Maybe that's why Dad works so much. The arguing hurts my ears, so of course he'd want to be far away from it, too.

Sometimes, Mom yells at me, too, because my eyes are green like Dad's and she doesn't want to see them.

But there's one thing that always makes me happy: our house has so many sunbirds in the front yard, with bright, blue-green heads. I always say, "Mom, Dad, look, the birds are back." They just ignore me or look at me weirdly, though. I guess they don't like them.

I remember one time Dad told me that Mom used to want to sing like a bird and dance in the sunlight, but she doesn't do it anymore. So maybe if Mom sings a little for Dad, then the arguments will stop, because that must've been what he loved about her.

So, while Dad is at work, I decide to ask her. She's in the kitchen, looking down at a pile of papers on the counter. Two sunbirds chirp at the window, near my fire lilies, and they're building a little nest.

"Mom, look at the birds. Don't they sound so nice?" Nothing. "Look, they—"

"Not now, Calvin. Mommy's busy."

"With what?" I push a stool and stand on it by the window and the counter where she is sitting. I can barely see the birds, but I imagine them hopping onto my hand. "Can I help?"

"No... sorry. It's grown-up stuff. And please don't look at me. I've seen enough of *him* already."

Then, the door opens; Dad's home. He looks tired, especially when he sees my birds. "Can I talk with you for a second, Marianne?" They walk deeper into the house, and I turn back to the birds. I can still hear Mom and Dad, but they aren't yelling.

I hear Dad say, "We need to do something about those birds. I'm tired of hearing Calvin talk about them, tired of hearing something in this household sing when you can't at all."

"Lowell, you're the one who had the great idea to make it big in the city, but—"

"I almost have it this time, I really do. I just want this one favor, please."

"Mom, Dad," I call out to them. "Look at the birds, they're building a nest together."

"But your son loves them," Mom says.

"Marianne, we don't know where those birds came from."

"Mom, Dad, look, the birds are doing everything together." I turn behind me and hear my stool scrape a bit. Why aren't they coming out?

"Just a minute, honey," Mom says. "Please, we have to put him first. He's the last thing we have, he's the only thing we have left that matters."

"Mom, Dad, look at the birds!" I try to step off the stool.

But then, I slip and fall headfirst on the stone counter. A sharp pain rips through my head, and everything goes black.

When I wake up, I'm in a pure white room in an uncomfy bed, and my parents are arguing in the hallway. Mom looks away from Dad, which is weird. She always tells me to look at whoever was speaking, because that's polite. Why does she want to be rude?

"I told you we had to do something about those birds," Dad says.

"Well, maybe if you paid a bit more attention to him, he wouldn't have hit his head."

"Why're you blaming me for this? He's *our* son."

I realize I have something on my head. What if I hit my head so hard, there was a giant hole in it, and they had to patch it up? I reach for it, but they both spot me and rush into the room.

"Calvin, don't touch your head."

"Calvin, don't."

I smile. "I'm fine, though. I'm just wondering what's on my head."

"Stitches," my dad says. "They help you heal. It'll be a few weeks, though."

The next day before I leave the hospital, my mom hums a little bit as she signs papers the doctors gave her. I can see what Dad meant—her hum sounds so free and happy.

"Don't tell Dad, but I think I'll sing for you two a little when we get back. I'm starting to remember why I loved to sing back then. I know you'll see, too."

Dad passes by her as she leaves to use the bathroom. I thought he would get angry hearing her still humming, but he says nothing until he sits down next to me.

"See what I mean? Her voice is beautiful. And Calvin, I'm sorry for talking so badly about your birds. When we get home, I'll make it up to you. And her."

When we get back, I don't hear any chirping. A little gray cat sniffs and scratches around the nest. "Hey, shoo, kitty-cat." I wave, and it runs off. I run to the nest. A little gray chick lies in the grass.

"Mom, Dad," I say. "This bird doesn't seem okay." I lift it up to show my dad.

"I don't think—" He breathes in. "Give me a moment, I'll get the trowels."

"I got it," Mom says as she passes two to him. I grab mine, but Dad's so surprised that he doesn't take his at first, so I start digging near the lilies under the window without him. "Come on, Dad."

"Oh. Right, let me help you with that." He takes the trowel and begins digging. "Actually, don't you think this bird should have a little box?"

"Yeah, I think it should. Mom, could you get a box?"

When she returns, Dad and I have already made a hole for the little bird, and I put it in the box. The sunbirds above me chirp a little as I put the chick inside.

"Maybe you should say something for it, Calvin."

I look up at the birds. The nest is torn apart. "I think its parents are already saying something for it, but..."

"It's not safe with that nest." We both look up to see Mom standing behind us. "They need a better home. I think we have some old carpentry back somewhere."

Dad and I spend the rest of the day making a new birdhouse.

I know it isn't the best looking home—the wood is a little too thin, and the roof is a little lopsided. But as dad helps me hold the hammer, I smile.

He and Mom, they aren't yelling for once, and I'm doing something with them, too. Mom watches us, and when I turn around, we look into each other's eyes.

She smiles. "You two are just like each other."

IMPERFECT FIT

by Kenneth Tran

the world is not meant for some people
like how clothes that fit some do not fit others
or how one's interests do not align with another's
yet, everyone is born into it and forced to survive
forced to fight for a success that may never come
a hopeless struggle with nature
a fruitless struggle with society
a timeless struggle with oneself
this is the reality of the world
the world that
is not meant for us

FRAYED ENDS

by Kathleen Vu

Do you remember
The day we first met?
Our first conversation,
And how we became friends?

You held me by the hand
And walked me to the nurse's office.
Not a single word spoken between us,
But I could never forget
The warmth of your hand.

Do you remember our first conversation?
It was a few days after.
You surprised me with balloons and a cupcake.
You joked, "Glad you're still alive."
And I joked back, "I'm too weird to die."
Ever since, we've been friends.

Remember the ice rink?
I kept falling, so you held my hand.
You were a better ice skater than I,
But the worst skating teacher ever.
Yet I could never forget
The warmth of your hand.

You stood by me since
The very beginning.
It's only natural I'd do the same.
After all, that's what best friends are for.

You made jokes about Narnia.
You never read the books
Nor watched any movies,
But I was the first to greet you
When you left Narnia.
I felt so honored and proud of you.

It was only a matter of time
Before you asked for my help.
I sewed together your rainbow cape
And watched as you ran around school
wearing that rainbow cape, finally free.

Do you remember when
You told me about your first crush?
Who knew you'd ask him out?
Maybe it's because I played a part,
I have always told you to be brave and free

It's so strange to see
Your best friend with a boyfriend.
And be so proud of the both of them
I could have felt
Angry or jealous
But you were so happy

Do you remember when
His mom made crocheted scarves?
You begged her to teach you.
Your boyfriend had no clue
That you wanted to make
A scarf of love, for love.

You were a fast learner,
I'd never seen you so happy.
You finished yours with ease,
But I couldn't finish my scarf,
I couldn't continue with the lessons.

You always asked me why I couldn't finish
My scarf left behind with frayed ends.
How could I tell you the truth?
It was more complex than the loops and stitches.

It took me years to
Understand the truth about myself.
I finally realized that
I could never finish my scarf
Because it couldn't be made for romantic love.

From the day we first met,
My feelings were so strong,
As strong as a ball of yarn.
As it unraveled, I looped
and stitched with my hooked needle.

The scarf grew longer as
Our friendship grew.
Then our friendship was so strong,
The scarf was almost finished.

I couldn't understand
Why my feelings, so strong from the start,
Became so weak and frayed.
Romantic love is so weird.

My love for you began romantic.
My love for you ended platonic.

It's about time I finish my scarf.
It can still be made of love,
It can be made for self-love instead.
Because self-love is really important
I'll keep the frayed ends.

There is a world for me.
It's only a matter of time
Before I leave Narnia.
You'll be the first to greet me

You left Narnia wearing a rainbow cape
Wait for me, my dearest loyal friend for
I will leave Narnia wearing
My finished scarf with frayed ends

BEING HUMAN

by Kenneth Tran

the radiance of deadly intent
the majestic display of unnatural bloodlust
everywhere and nowhere

let your mind drift here
in this state, in the ambience of a floating cloud
mist caressing your body
sticking onto your skin
forming small drops of water
they trickle

and like all things, they fall
the nerves in your body shake
the soul collapses
an ecstasy beyond belief

i am in that state
if the floating cloud
was the heart of a flaming phoenix
if the concept of ecstasy
was one of despair

a truly crippling master
suffocating
burning
trapped outside heaven's gate
i am in that state
and so i am every single day

LOSING LEAVES

by Shannon Le

Branches hung over the lake
with a current that swept away debris.
The shrubs fought to stay
stiff and crisp, denying that
the change in the season had begun.

The wrinkled and knotted trees,
however, acknowledged the bitter wind.
Leaves scattered on the grass,
mottled and bruise-colored.

Even though tree branches bent
to weep for the leaves
parting from them,
their stony trunks stayed resolute.

A model boat on the lake
with the same steely resilience
sailed on murky waters,
even when it had been abandoned.

The boat passed under a cedar bridge,
chipped and worn,
as the winds of time drifted in.
Autumn slowly stole everything,
yet nature took the loss
in perfect grace.

SENTIENT BEINGS

by Benson Truong

Humans were made to feel pain,
it runs through our cold dark veins,
blood pumps from the heart to the brain,
what a repetitive process it has to sustain.

Over time the heart weakens, becoming dry and stale,
it is headed off on a one path journey destined to fail,
if only there was someone to save me before the storms assail,
two star crossed lovers, the manifestation of a brand new fairytale.

She introduced herself during my adolescent years,
ensuring me together we would tackle our greatest fears.
her brightly lit smile shone far and wide,
acting as the famous lodestar, my one and only guide.

My heart was shattered like a broken glass cup,
but you came and carefully glued it all back up.
My heart was hollowed, abandoned, and emptied,
but you came and filled it back with your empathy.

Were you my saint, sent from the heavens,
here to fulfill me with your blessings?
we were perfectly crafted,
there was no way this love could be disastrous.

But alas, this infatuation didn't last,
you walked out on me, turning me into a lonely outcast.
The sudden news left me shocked and aghast,
how did I let this opportunity slip right past?

You're no angel, you're a wicked witch,
who dug a deep hole, throwing me into a dry black ditch.
Why couldn't you love me right,
all you chose to do was to bicker and fight.

Here I am, back at square one,
suffering from boundless pain and feeling stunned,
I might have to drown out all my sorrows,
until I can find another heart to borrow.

WORDS

by Kimbill Ly

The vernacular vocabulary volunteers to vilify and vex
viciously as if a volatile volcano vomited vindictively
Its vulgar vice vandalizes our hearts, Victimizing with vanity
With disregard for vulnerability
Words are no virtue, only viruses voyaging like vultures in the sky,
Veering towards vulgarity instead of valence, very visible,
Vengeful venom vigorously voicing verbs and profanity
And yet we still listen
And yet we still talk
We choose to pick the prose
We choose to speak the speech,
confidently undermining confidence
All for a slight sliver of satisfaction
Our slurs are serrated, they slice souls and smile with similes,
Sarcastically saluting sadness and sorrow
Silly me, words are not at fault
The voice that wills the words without wisdom is to blame
For wildly washing over the worried and
Weaving in words until the line gets blurry

ALWAYS SPIRALING, NEVER ENDING

by Darby Vaughn

Tick Tock Tick
The sound of a clock rings,
Never stopping, never pausing.
Tock Tick Tock
Write, draw, play.
Yet why still,
Do the things that I love most,
Seem like a chore rather than a pleasure?
Is it the projects?
Is it the assignments?
Have I lost my love for drawing and writing?
Or is it the insistent nagging in my head
That just tells me to work?
Tick Tock Tick
Where is the passion?
Where is the love?
Was there any of that to begin with,
Or did I always stress over such minute details?
Tock Tick Tock.

BREAKING POINT

by Christine Vu

YASU'S HEELS ECHOED IN the classroom. She stopped in front of Alberto. Her eyes bore down on him, hunched over his phone.

"Alberto," Yasu raised her voice, "Where are your data notes for the lab?"

Alberto mouthed out an exclamation as his eyes widened. "Yeah, I have them." He ran a finger through his magenta-streaked hair, as one earbud fell out. "Wait, I think I left them at home."

"I asked about them last night," Yasu said. "Didn't you get my email?"

Alberto shrugged and slunk down into the chair next to her. "Sorry about that."

Ms. Eichel shut the classroom door. "Hopefully you and your partner have all of your lab notes today, so you can share your data. You'll transfer that data to your lab report which you'll be writing individually. Remember, this is due at the end of the period. Go ahead and get out your Chromebooks."

Everybody retrieved their notes and their Chromebooks. That is, everybody who had their notes.

"Hey, you still have your notes from yesterday, right?" Alberto leaned over to Yasu.

She rolled her eyes. "Of course I do." She retrieved her part of their lab notes and set them down. "But I'm using them first."

"Alright, I'll wait."

Yasu returned to her screen and typed up a base structure for her lab report. She then transferred her notes. They only took up a third of the page.

That won't be good enough.

She looked at Alberto. He sat there with an expectant smile. She sighed and handed over her notes.

"Thanks," he said.

"I'll need them back."

She continued her lab report with what she already knew. It didn't fill the page as much as she'd hoped. She frowned. Of course, that's because Alberto had the other half of the needed data.

She glanced over at him. He was typing just as fast as everybody else.

Whatever. She already had everything she needed. Unless…

She reread her lab report. There was a term missing. She should know this. She wrote it down the other day, after all. She reread that sentence twice. But what was it?

She glanced at the clock and bit her lip. How was class already halfway over?

What if it'll come to her?

She reread the last thing she wrote and continued from there. A couple sentences later, she stopped short. What was that technique called again?

Her eyes searched the classroom. Nothing relevant.

The clock above ticked.

This should be easy. It should still be fresh in her memory. Everything was done yesterday, after all.

But not everything was done; Alberto had to finish his part last night. He had half the key pieces.

Those were the key pieces her sparse report was in dire need of.

Could she finish without them? Of course not, a lab report without half of the data would be incomplete. What if she explained them vaguely? No, she'd look incompetent.

The clock ticked again.

Her cursor flickered between the save button and the progress. All she could hear was the clicking and tapping in front of her. Around her. Next to her. Behind her.

Somebody's watch beeped. Yasu blinked. She recognized that. That cue.

A few students around her unzipped their backpacks and tucked away binders. Fifteen minutes left until class ends.

Yasu reread her report from the beginning. Maybe she overlooked something. Maybe the answer was there all along.

Another tick of the clock. Louder than before.

Her finger dragged down on the scroll wheel. No results.

More ticking. Never before had the clock ticked so loud. Rummages and rustling around Yasu escalated.

She swallowed.

"Ten minutes remaining," Ms. Eichel announced.

To Yasu, everything else that followed muffled out.

"Five minutes remaining," Ms. Eichel announced.

Yasu breathed in and out. Why can't she just finish the report? She kept hitting the save button more times than she could keep track of, despite lack of any real progress made. Her lips tightened.

"Yasu, Ms. Eichel said to return the Chromebooks," Alberto said. "We're not leaving until they're all put away."

No, no, no. She always finished everything. On time and well-informed. Always. She can't *not* finish.

"Oh my god, what is she doing?" a passing classmate said.

The clock ticked once more. What was that? Did she miss something?

"Come on, we only have a few minutes left," Alberto said.

Yasu's fingers fumbled as she snuck in last minute words. She navigated her mouse to the Save button, but misclicked. Her cursor hit Submit. A loading wheel appeared.

No. Why? She wasn't done.

The screen changed. It went through. Yasu slammed her Chromebook shut.

Shoulders heaved and fists balled, Yasu collapsed over her desk.

Alberto gingerly picked up her Chromebook. "I'll put this away for you," he whispered.

Someone's watch beeped again.

Without missing a beat, Yasu shoved her papers and stationery off the desk. Highlighters and mechanical pencils clattered. A spiral notebook skidded across the vinyl floor. A high-pitch frequency echoed in her head. Everything scattered about her.

Students gasped.

"Yasu?" A voice reached her ears and Yasu directed her attention to the source. Her lips parted.

Ms. Eichel stood in front of the Chromebook cart. The teacher's aide stood next to her with his arms crossed.

Yasu released a ragged breath. She lowered her gaze to the scene before her.

She glanced back up. All eyes were on her. Her lip quivered.

What have I done?

Without thinking, her legs guided her outside the door. She didn't realize where she was until the sunlight hit her face.

Her feet slowed down and she staggered over to a bench, brought her knees to her chest, and buried her eyes in her arms.

Slow footsteps shuffled nearby.

"Yasu?" a student said with a soft voice.

Yasu looked up. Oh, the teacher's assistant.

"I'm Evan," he said, sitting down next to her. "I thought you could use a friend."

Yasu lifted her head. "What do you mean?"

"I mean, someone else to—" He stopped and opened his jacket. He pulled out a green journal and held it in front of Yasu. "I noticed you don't seem to have anybody to turn to."

She shifted herself to fully face him. "Pardon me?"

Evan opened his journal. "You could use someone to talk to."

He pointed at one entry. "Sometimes, I don't know how to think. So my parents suggested that I slow down, and I found writing helps. I didn't understand what I was doing at first, but then I made sense of it."

Each entry started the same. Incoherent scribbles and gibberish that developed into words. Single words that grew into short sentences. Then longer sentences by the end of the paragraph.

"I think you should try it." He smiled at Yasu. "You may not get it now, but you will later."

Yasu took the book and observed it for a moment then looked at Evan. His smile seemed genuine.

He held out his pen to her. "You can write in it, I don't mind."

Yasu slowly accepted the pen and held the journal closer to her. She flipped to an empty page. The pen hovered over the first line. It never touched down.

"It doesn't matter if the first thing makes no sense. Write the first word in your mind and your hand will keep up," Evan said. His smile softened, and he didn't fidget or retreat.

In shaky cursive, she wrote the first word in her mind.

Breaking.

Evan craned his neck. His hand reached down, next to hers.

With his own pen, he added:

But not broken.

HELLO MORNING

by Andrea Torres

Abstract colors of the sun
awaken me.
I gaze out my window
with sleepy eyes.
A brand new day awaits me.
Warm orange, gentle pink.
Those familiar colors
associated with dawn.
Let me breathe in the crisp air
Let me bask in the daylight
For a new day
starts with greeting the familiar sky.
Animals sing
Songs of new beginnings and new days
Out of bed I get.
Clothes wrapped around me.
Out to meet with this familiar sky.

BEAST IN THE CITY

by Vi Bui

A lonely midnight stroll
Beyond the path most taken
City lights line the streets, the theater is about to open
Dancing among the leaves caught in the breeze
Evil lurks backstage, waiting for its cue
Following the prey, like a fox in a stone garden
Going for the kill, an actor's final bow
Hiding behind a mask, playing a character, wearing a facade
In an alley where no men tread, a stage awaits a play
Just as the clock strikes two, the finale commences
Kill the lights, kill the show, kill the showman
Leave behind streaks of crimson, reel in the red curtains,
　　pick up the ruby roses
Mindless terror, meaningless violence, momentary ecstasy
Now there's nothing left, except the shadow against the wall
Over the spotlight, the stars flicker on and off
People clap, people gasp, the performance is over
Quiet settles over, ridged breaths fall stagnant
Run, run, run off stage
Smile, be proud of your work, look at what you've done
The show is over, there's no reason to laugh
Under the street lamps, under the cover of night
Venom drips from your mouth, lies you spit like a snake
Who could've stopped this, no one but yourself
Xysti can't hide the crime, everyone will know of the performance
You're to blame, You're at fault
Zip your lips and hope no one will know

OLD SUMMER DAYS

by Cattu Do

The summer days were
radiant from the hot sun.
You would come early
with a bag of fun,
a small blanket,
and extra clothes.
It was as if you lived in my home,
like a part of my family,
my other half.
The room always filled with
laughter from our silly jokes.
When the sun came down,
we sat on a hill, shared our little secrets.
Those memories will never disappear.
We crossed our hearts,
and hoped to die,
with our secrets hidden underneath our lives.
It was the little memories,
that made you so valuable.
The sun came up every day,
we didn't know at the time,
that there'd be a day when it would not come.
And as time passes by, day by day,
I know these memories will always stay.

HOW I MET YOU

by Cattu Do

The gush of hot wind,
The summer waves heating the floor,
There you were, there I was,
And there we met—under a tree,

It wasn't supposed to be a special day,
But it was a day that was unexpected,
Where it started—where we left it,
When we turned around and made it all happen,

It wasn't so long ago,
Four years have passed—but four years happened,
We may have stopped looking—something once was there,
We distanced from what was once so pure,

Many memories made, many have faded,
I guess you really can't take back what has washed away,
So I'll stand strong for not only you and me,
I'll stand here to tell you that we need to let it be,

For something to become better, for something that might be
greater,
We shall take our time—making this our last cycle,
We will take chances—through these tough moments,
To recreate something that was once full of happiness.

FAKE SMILE

by Kady Tran

You go on like everything is okay
Like these problems will never come rushing back
Like a heavy tidal wave that'll eat you alive
The way the guilt will continue to do so
You go on and put on that fake smile
But no matter how hard you try,
It's never going to hide that guilty frown of yours

And you know that it was wrong
You know that you can't forget what you did
So you hide in the shadows
Because you're afraid you'll be recognized in the light
But no matter where you run,
You could never escape the horrors beyond your version of reality

Behind those pale brown eyes and sweet strawberry blonde hair,
You hide your broken self
This facade you put on fools everyone
Until they see you cry
They see that there's more to you
Than those freckles and bubbly personality

You carry a deep hatred that will haunt you forever
It lingers and crawls underneath your skin
It frightens you during the night
But just when you think those fears wash away in the light,
It silently follows you

It taunts you, it screams at you, it cries at you
You think you can block out the heavy noises
Truthfully, you hear it
And you cry and scream back at it

The feeling is so familiar,
It's called guilt

I hope that the guilt hits you like a ton of bricks
The way you did to me with no hesitation
You think that I'm gone forever
But am I really?
I will forever haunt you
And the guilt you carry with you
Will weigh you down
Just like bricks.

SEA OF SAND

by Bryce Le

EVERYTHING WAS DRY. So, so, dry. The sun blazed overhead, its heat furiously beating on the ground. The sand dunes stretched onwards towards infinity, an endless desert that consumed the entire world. I stumbled forward to an uncertain destination. For several days now, I had been going in this direction.

There was nothing, nothing but the endless sea of gilded dust. Even the sky was empty and the wind was frozen in time.

Where were the people?

Where were the buildings?

What happened to everything?

Eventually, I lost track of just how far I traveled. When I glanced back at my path, the trail of footprints went on forever, until the ripples in the desert air obscured them. I didn't even know how long I had been here for. The lengths of the days and nights change at random, and the only constant is the fact that the day is always *much* longer than the night. I lost count of the days, but I was sure I had seen at least several thousand pass by. And so, I trekked onwards through the sand. It was subconscious at this point; my body just moved by itself, continuing on the path I set.

Until one day, something finally changed. I noticed a shadowed figure standing in the distance, looking directly at me. Without another thought, I turned and made a beeline for it. It could have been a murderous cannibal for all I cared. I needed some human company, something that could prove I wasn't alone. As I neared the figure, the details cleared, no longer obscured by the ripples in the air.

The first thing I noticed was his oversized hat. Seriously, it was almost four feet in diameter. In what situation would you even need a hat that big? Unless, of course, you found yourself stuck in an endless desert where there were no clouds and a day seemed to stretch on for several times longer than it should have. That was kind of an edge case, though.

He strolled towards me, his shoulders back, head held high. It was like he was having a nice walk in the park compared to my unsteady trudging through the sand. More features came into view as he neared. A cowboy vest covered a red plaid shirt. His faded blue jeans looked torn apart and sewn back together several times. He stopped in front of me and stared, before opening his mouth.

His voice washed over me, a lazy drawl that was surprisingly soft, considering its source. It was the first word I had heard in ages. "Never seen your face before. You new?"

I nodded, mind reeling over the fact that there was somebody else here, that I was meeting with a real person for the first time since I got to this desert. "Where…?" My voice rasped from years of dehydration and disuse.

Luckily, he understood what I had in mind. He handed me his canteen and began to speak.

"Well, long story short, this is Purgatory. It's where all the lost souls go, those who couldn't make it to Heaven because they weren't good, but didn't go to Hell because they weren't evil either. I'd give you a tour, but…" He rubbed the back of his head and glanced around. "There ain't much to show. And the only things that *are* worth showing move around all the time, so there's no point—" he cut himself off, leaning closer towards me.

Did I do something wrong? I didn't think so. All I did was stand there. He furrowed his brow.

"You… are not dead."

Well, if I wasn't dead, then how did I end up here? He noticed my growing confusion and began to explain.

"Don't worry, we get your type every once in a while. Folks who lost something and want to find it again, mostly. I don't often recommend it, but it's not my place to get in the way." He shook his head and pinched the bridge of his nose, as if trying to repress a bad memory. "I'm curious, though. What are you looking for?"

It was a good question. Why was I here?

I attempted to summon up the memories of my past, my mind racing as I considered the question. It couldn't have been an object; I was never a materialistic person. Nor could it have been an animal, since I never had any pets. Out of all the options I could think of, a person sounded the most correct, but I felt that there was something… *wrong* with that idea, like it wasn't the person itself, but something *from* them.

But what was it? And from who?

"Don't know, eh?" He smiled at me. "Not a problem. Most other folks aren't sure either. You'll figure it out eventually, no need to worry."

"What now?" It wasn't like walking around in the middle of nowhere had helped me out so far.

"Just keep walkin', I suppose."

I stared at him blankly.

"Don't look at me like that. I ain't really sure how it works either. You'll have to ask some of the folks who've been here longer than me."

"Alright."

He turned to leave, before glancing back. "Almost forgot. 'Fore you go, let me give you some advice."

"What?"

"One of the main rules here. If you're alive, don't eat anything. Drink all you want, but just make sure to never eat."

"Why?"

"Well, do you remember any of those Greek myths from Earth? About the afterlife?"

I nodded. "Like how Persephone ate the fruit and got stuck in the underworld, right?"

"Well, that's basically what happens whenever you eat anything here."

"Oh."

"That's all I got to say. Good luck finding whatever it is you're looking for." The man tipped his hat and departed. I watched him stroll away, his massive hat bobbing up and down before he disappeared over a dune.

And I was alone again.

I sighed. Time to continue with the exciting desert trek through the middle of nowhere with no landmarks or stops. My legs moved rhythmically on the sand, carrying my body forward with every step. One foot up, one foot down. One foot up, one foot down. On and on I carved a path through the endless sand, all the while thinking about what the man had told me. I paused. I never got his name. Well, it wasn't like I was going to be seeing him again anyway.

But the things he said stayed in my mind. What was I looking for? Once more, I attempted to force the memory from the depths of my mind. But every time I neared the answer, something blocked me. Perhaps I needed more time.

I trudged onward, the days and nights flying by as I made steady progress towards… something. I wasn't sure.

Hundreds of days passed while I continued to wander amongst the dunes. I never stopped, not for a break or for sleep, until I spotted something far away. A beam of light shining in the sky, cutting its way through the darkness and reaching me. Finally, something new. And this time, it was in the same direction that I was heading. As I crested the hill, it came into view.

A massive building stood several stories tall and was adorned with marble pillars. From its windows, a soft orange glow seeped out, filling the area with a comforting aura. A woman in a blue dress stood in front of the entrance, face adorned with a bright smile. As her eyes swept over the landscape, she caught sight of me and hurried over.

"Oh dear," she said. "Darling, you look a mess. Come on, get inside," she said as she dragged me by the arm into the building.

"What is this?" I said. Why was it here?

"The 'what' doesn't matter right now, dear. What matters is that you look dead tired." She continued to lead through the doorway and up a flight of stairs. "I've got a bed and a warm shower here if you need them, darling. Get some rest." She pushed me into the room. "We'll talk in the morning."

I was too tired to protest, and besides, it was impolite to refuse kindness. I walked into the bathroom and turned on the shower, waiting for it to heat up before stepping in.

Sure, it was a bit odd finding what seemed to be a massive hotel in the middle of this desert. But the more I thought about it, the less it seemed to matter. Of course there would be a hotel here. It made just about as much sense as the rest of the desert, so why shouldn't it be here?

I stumbled over to the bed, before collapsing upon it. I never realized just how *tired* I was until then. My eyes closed, and I drifted off to sleep.

It was the first rest I had in years.

I woke up to the morning sunlight hitting me directly in the eyes, causing me to roll over and off the bed. Ouch. That was one way to get up in the morning. I rose from the ground and brushed myself off, stepping out into the hall. Music drifted up the staircase, a jaunty, somewhat scratchy piano tune. I walked down to the first floor, where the woman was sitting at a pristine marble countertop.

"Come here, dear. You look famished. I'll cook something up for you. How do you feel about some bacon and eggs?"

I sat down near the counter, and I was about to accept, before I remembered what the man from before told me. *"Don't eat anything. Drink all you want, but just make sure to never eat any food."*

"Just water, thank you," I said.

"Really, darling. I do think you should have *something*. You look like you're starving."

"I'm fine."

"Come now dear, you can't seriously tell me you're not hungry at all. Have you seen yourself?" she said, pulling out a hand mirror. "Go on, have a look, darling."

She held the mirror up to my face. I glanced into it and—*man* I looked awful. Sunken cheeks, dried skin, dark bags. I looked like someone who had just gone a few years without food, probably because I did just that. I was thinner than a stick. Actually, "stick" was generous; "twig" was more like it.

"See what I mean?" She leaned closer to me. "Have some food, darling. It'll make it all better."

Maybe she was right. I *was* feeling hungry, to say the least. Besides, one bite wouldn't hurt, right?

No. I slapped myself mentally. The man had told me to not eat food for a reason, and he had a cool hat, so he had to be right. I glanced away from the mirror and—how was there suddenly food in front of me? The lady hadn't even moved. She was still staring expectantly at me, eyes flickering between my face and the plate of eggs.

It was probably a good idea for me to leave before I got anymore funny ideas. I rose from my chair. "Thank you for the hospitality, ma'am, but I really have to get going—"

"Nonsense, dear." She grabbed my shoulder and pulled, forcing me back down into the seat. "Go on, eat up." I tried to remove myself from her grip, but she only held on tighter.

This wasn't good. "I'm not dead yet, ma'am. I shouldn't eat—"

"I know."

Oh dear.

The greatest threat that I faced in Purgatory was a lady trying to feed me breakfast. Who would have thought? I had to get out of here. I did *not* want to be stuck walking around a desert forever. I had things to do, damn it. I still had to meet her.

Wait. *Her?* Where did that come from?

This probably wasn't the best time for introspection. I had time to think about it later. There was still a possibly evil woman attempting to trap me in Purgatory using bacon and eggs, and that was not a sentence that I had ever expected to say. I racked my brain for a possible escape route. The door was still open, so all I had to do was slip out of her vice-like grip.

"These eggs do look quite appetizing…" I began. The woman's eyes lit up. "But I'd like a drink to go with them."

"Not a problem, darling. Wait right here." She released my arm and got up.

I can't believe that actually worked.

As soon as she turned away, I bolted for the door, fleeing from the building. I was free. I wouldn't be cursed to wander the desert for eternity. Instead I would wander around the desert for an undefined amount of time, possibly eternity. Maybe that didn't make much of a difference at all.

Now then, who exactly was the "*her*" that I was thinking about earlier? Once again, I dug deep into my memories. Only a single new image appeared in my mind. A woman, with black hair and dark brown eyes, smiling softly at me. No background, no context, nothing but a smile. What made this smile so important?

The building disappeared over a dune. I continued forward. I'd find it eventually. I'd find *her* eventually. If not for anything else, then for answers.

Time flew by, but her image stayed in the front of my mind. As I wandered over dunes and through valleys, I never stopped thinking about it. Who was she? How did I know her?

More importantly, what did I want from her?

With those questions in mind, I journeyed onwards across the desert, the sun hanging high in the sky. For another hundred or so days, I continued, until I heard something that stopped me in my tracks.

"Hey, wait up," a voice called out from behind me. I barely had time to turn around before something slammed into my back, sending both of us tumbling down a hill. I glanced down to see what hit me. A teenage girl pushed herself off the ground.

Black hair. My breath hitched.

Amber eyes. It wasn't her.

"Sorry about that," the girl said. "It's just been a while since I've seen anyone."

Her voice was high and breathy, almost like she just finished running a marathon—which was probably close to the truth, considering the long trail of footprints behind her.

"You alright?" she asked, reaching out a hand. I accepted it, and she pulled me to my feet.

"Yeah, I'm fine," I said. "What about you?"

"Don't worry about me, I'm tougher than I look. But I wanted to ask…"

"Yes?"

"You're... still alive, right? Just like me?" she asked, twirling her hair around her fingers.

"Yes." I managed to conceal my excitement at meeting someone else like me. At least, I think I did.

Her stance relaxed. "That's good. Would've been kind of embarrassing if I was wrong. Well, since you're alive, do you know what you're looking for?"

"It's... a person. A woman, I think. That's all I know."

"Well, at least you've got that much. I still have no idea what I'm supposed to be here for." She frowned.

"Have you been able to find anything out about this place, at least?"

"Not much. I've been here for a while, but to be honest, most of that was just me aimlessly wandering around." She rubbed her head and appeared to be thinking deeply on something. Her eyes lit up. "I know this lady who's been here *way* longer than me. She probably knows more than I do." She smiled. "Want to meet her?"

"I see no reason not to."

"Alright then, follow me," the girl said. She lifted her foot, turned around, and marched back the way she came. I followed along, contributing little to her jaunty whistling, and together, we trekked across the desert. Compared to my previous journeys, this one was quite short in comparison. It only took a few dozen days instead of a few hundred. Perks of having someone who actually knows where they're going, I suppose. Of course, being the paragon of sociability that I was, I said absolutely nothing to her on the trip despite her many attempts at asking me questions. It was rather nice to have company for once, though. We crested a ridge and feasted our eyes on a large pond, palm trees growing around its edges.

No fair. Other people get a fancy, peaceful oasis while I get a lady who tries to force feed me? There's no justice in the world.

"She should be here." We walked down the hill, stopping once we reached the shade of a palm tree.

"Nice place," I said, admiring the fronds and the pond in the center.

She smiled. "Well, Purgatory can't be *all* desert. There's got to be some things to break it up every now and then."

"I thought being boring was Purgatory's thing."

"And I thought 'being quiet' was yours, but here we are."

We continued looking around the oasis.

"So... this person knows a lot, right?" I asked her. "If she knows a lot, and you've talked to her, then why don't you know a lot?"

She gave me a mild glare, before sighing. "I do know a lot. It's just that none of those things are the thing that I'm looking for."

"Maybe you just need to think deep into your memories."

"Wow, what good advice. It's almost like I haven't been trying that for years." She chuckled. "Look, there she is," the girl said, pointing to the shore of the pond. My gaze followed her arm.

And I saw *her*.

The girl noticed my expression. "Do you know her?" She asked me.

"She seems… familiar," I responded. She was more than familiar. She was seared into my mind, a person that I could never forget. But why?

"Really?" She turned to me. I nodded. "...Well, I don't want to get in the way of a reunion. Good luck with her." She turned and began to walk away.

"Thank you," I said. She gave no indication that she heard me, simply walking over a hill, disappearing into the sands. I turned back and faced *her*.

The woman and I continued to stare at each other, unblinking. I realized now what I wanted.

An apology, or maybe an accusation. Possibly even a mixture of both. Perhaps it was just an average conversation that we never got to finish, something as simple as a discussion about a book. There were infinite possibilities, but they always boiled down to the same thing.

Closure. That was what I was looking for.

"I didn't think I'd see you again." The words I held inside for so long now came out easily. "You always hid your burdens behind a smile. The last thing I wanted to do was make it worse. So I kept everything to myself. But now I remember how you'd appear in my dreams, before I'd startle awake. I was afraid that you died thinking I didn't care." I sighed. "I'm sorry for never saying enough. I took you for granted."

She simply smiled, making the same face that was etched into my memory, and nodded. No words came out of her mouth, but I understood. Everything would be okay.

It was time for me to go.

GRAFFITI

by An Huynh

we paint on the walls for all to see,
expressing our hopes and dreams
we scream out our individuality
with red, yellow, and green

but they call us rebels
and look down on our art
they trash the blues and blacks of our hearts
and tear our thoughts apart

yet we continue to paint
to dare, to show that we care
spilling our true colors everywhere
and making them all aware

that we were there

DREAMERS

by Emily Kieu

We often spend our days at home,
Lying in bed, over-sleeping, and playing Animal Crossing.
Sometimes, I miss the days I took for granted.
I miss the sun shining on my pale face.
I miss the late-night drives with my friends.
I miss the days when I'm at school.
I sometimes imagine if I would even have a prom night.
I can only watch the sky from a distance.
I look through my Instagram or Snapchat,
Through posts of the days when everything was great,
When we were living our teenage dream.
I wish I didn't take these things for granted because now,
All I can do is patiently wait.
To once again step my toes in the grainy sand,
To watch the sunset with my boyfriend.
If only I knew, beforehand.

LETTER TO ORPHEUS

by Colleen King

You promised me love
You promised me safety
With your words, and your poetry, and your lyrics
You said you'd keep walking
And listen for the steps behind you
Did you not hear me?
Did the doubt overcome your mind
And force your body to betray
What your heart knew was true?
Doubt that clouds the mind
Doubt that clouds the soul
Doubt that no promise of love
Or safety
Can ever protect and hold.
Destined to be soulmates
But lost to the flames of the Underworld.
Lost to the doubt
That I was not following you all along.
You turned to make sure I was there
But you didn't trust yourself,
Or King Hades, or Lady Persephone,
And decided to trust the doubt
Inside your head.

YET SHE STAYS

by Colleen King

Anemia makes her weak, yet
Blissful.
Careful she is to not wake the sleeping creature who
Dares her to fall asleep at night.
Even so,
False hopes of
God and
Heaven
Ignite in her heart.
Just enough to
Keep her faith
Living.
Menacing monsters
Need her essence.
Oaths of fake love make her stay.
Poised with her chin high,
Questions rise in her head.
Reasons why she should stay,
          and reasons why she shouldn't.
Still, she remains
To care for the creature who's become dear to her heart.
Understand that this is no human she deals with, but a
Vampire
Weakening her spirit.
Xerotic is her heart.
Yet she stays there,
Zombifying what's left of humanity in her.

FOR YOU

by Michelle Lam

If I were a flower
Your fingers would find
Velvet petals soft to the touch
I would smell sickeningly sweet
And overwhelm your senses
Enchanting and enticing you.
I'm sorry that I am but a spiny weed
Crawling over the garden
Suffocating the other flowers you love
Just to reach out and offer you
A dandelion

WHEN IT FALLS

by Terry Nguyen

Even through it all
I still don't see us as a fall
We're constant
That's unfortunate
Happy times need sad times
Sad times need happy times
Going from as high as a cliff
To a painful fall
New friends, I caught them
Old friends, I lost them
During this time, also known as autumn
Is when I start to reminisce what I saw
As everything around me, except
autumn, falls

MY VERY BEST FRIEND

by Vi Bui

CALEB RAN THROUGH THE school halls, narrowly colliding with his classmates to get to the club meeting room. He knew he would be late after football practice, but he couldn't let his team down. He sped by the hall monitor, made a sharp turn to the right, and stumbled over his own feet as he slid across the tiled floor. He stopped in front of the door with a sign neatly taped up. "Welcome to the Board Game Club!"

He burst through the door with a bang. "I'm here, Janice." He nearly collapsed onto the door frame as the club president turned around.

"Hey, Cale—oh, you look like a mess." Without follow up, Janice set plastic chairs near the table. She set a box down and unpacked its contents: numerous small tokens, plastic figures and dice, cheap pencils, and a worn board. "Anyway, take a seat so we can get this meeting rolling."

"Hey, don't be so rude to your only club member. We wouldn't even have this room if—"

"Shhh." She pressed her finger to her smile. "It's our secret so don't say it too loud." She walked over and closed the door behind him. "You're lucky no one's around."

Caleb sat down and rubbed his hands together. "So what are we playing today?" he said as he moved the chair closer and looked at the game.

"Chess, like usual. Can you fill out the paper for me?" Janice motioned to the clipboard on the edge of the table, an unfilled sheet attached to it.

Caleb grabbed the board, whipped out a pencil and scanned the paper. It asked for the information that a real club would care about. He wrote down made-up names and random phone numbers that would seem believable for a small club, standard procedure. Since no one really paid attention to Board Game Club, everything would be taken as the truth.

"So, ready to play?"

"Heck yeah I am, but are *you* ready? 'Cause I'm bringing my A-game."

Hours passed as the two sat in the room, all alone with themselves and a chess board. Despite being under the administration's radar, everyone knew about the Board Game Club and its two dedicated members. Even after all the other members drifted away, Caleb and Janice insisted on keeping it alive; their love of gaming was too strong to take them down. Which is why rumors had spread around the halls.

"Think they're dating?" someone would whisper.

"Duh, of course," another would reply. "Why else would a girl and a boy spend so much time together?" Both would nod and leave it at that. No one would ask Caleb or Janice outright—there wasn't a reason to.

Their game slowed down, both at their wits' ends. While waiting for the next move, Caleb asked, "You going to the dance?"

Janice rubbed her chin. "No."

"Me neither." He watched as she moved her knight and smirked. With a flick of her wrist, she knocked down his queen. "I wish I could though," he whispered. An uncomfortable silence filled the room as Caleb took his sweet time on his turn.

Janice held her breath and bounced her leg as she watched. "I have an idea," she blurted.

"Wait your turn, silly."

"No, not the game. The dance." She crossed her legs as she leaned closer to him.

"Hold up." Caleb continued to stare at the board until his hand moved forward his pawn. "Okay, lay it on me. What's up?"

"What if we help each other get dates?" She waited for a reaction.

"That sounds," he turned his head up, "dumb."

Janice frowned.

"I'm not a good wingman and neither are you. Remember last year?"

"Don't remind me." She shuddered. "But trust me, this time will be better. Promise. This time it's mutual friends, so they're bound to agree."

"I don't follow, chief. What do you mean by mutual friends?" Caleb sat up straight. "Does someone we know like me? And what about you? Does someone like you?"

"Yeah, someone likes you. As for me…" A shy smile crept across Janice's face.

"My best friend has a crush and didn't tell me?" He gasped in overdramatic outrage. "I thought we had something special."

She pouted. "I had to keep it a secret. Otherwise you'd run off to the nearest radio station and tell the whole town. I know you like the back of a game box."

"I see your point now. Good call, but the elephant still stands."

She curled up in her chair and looked away as her cheeks turned cherry red. "Do I have to say it?" He nodded, and she scratched her cheek. "It's… Brody."

"Brody." Caleb pressed his lips together hesitantly before continuing. "That's great. I can see you two together."

"Shut up. Someone might hear you, idiot. You're making me blush just by thinking about it." Her hands shot up to cup her burning face.

"Sorry. Didn't mean to embarrass you." He leaned back down. "Why him though? I thought you'd be into someone like yourself. Headstrong and stubborn. Or a bookworm, with thick old glasses, you've always liked cute guys."

"Meh, they're all so, not to be rude, boring. I need someone with ideas, not someone who just reads them. And Brody's just that kind of guy. "

"Brody's a great guy from what I know, but how do you know him? You're not a sporty person."

"Debate club, he's super involved in that. I mean, have you heard him argue in the halls? He could step on a soapbox on the corner of the road and run the mayor out of town. Had a fair share of arguments with that guy."

"Wow, I had no clue. I think we got a solid candidate here."

"Yeah…" Janice rubbed her arm. "I just hope he feels the same way."

"So who's into me? I can't imagine anyone wants to take me out."

"What? Dude, you're the nicest person I know." It was her turn to look offended. "And not just normal-nice, but saint-like. Remember that kitten?"

"Aww." His eyes lit up. "She bit me a ton but turned out to be a real cutie."

"And don't forget, you're on the football team and everybody likes a buff boy. You're the second most datable person in this whole school as far as I know."

He raised a brow. "Well, if you think I'm so great, why don't you date me yourself?"

Complete silence entered the room. Caleb didn't say anything else. Janice didn't respond, but then a smirk curled up. As quickly as the room fell quiet, it was filled with the bursting laughter of the two. Unable to contain themselves, their laughing only stopped when they coughed and gasped for air. They took deep breaths to return to reality and Janice checked the clock.

"Hey, school closes in less than ten minutes, so it's a draw." She turned towards Caleb and smiled. "For now. Pack up the pieces, I'll fold the board."

"Aye, aye Captain." He saluted and got to work clearing off the desk. As his hands swiped across the table, he looked up. "You never answered me, though. Who wants to go out with me?"

Her eyes were glued to the game box. "Oh, it's Marilyn from chemistry. She thinks you're super cool and she has a thing for strong men. That fits your description perfectly."

"Wait, how will we know if I like her? I've never even talked to her."

"Oh yeah, what's your type again?"

"Uh, I don't know. My age?"

"That's not—see, this is why you have to ask. Can't have a favorite if you've never had a taste. We have to start somewhere, and wouldn't you like to make a girl's dream come true?"

Caleb leaned his head on his hand. "I didn't think about that. Seems weird she wants to date me but doesn't even talk to me. How does she know what I'm like?"

She looked him in the eye. "Seriously, have you ever had a crush? You're the only person in the world who would think that. Also, you read like an open book. You wear your heart on your sleeve. It's not too hard to get the gist of who you are."

"Whatever man. Don't call me out. Besides, when are we asking them out? The dance is this Friday."

"Yeah, that means we have…" She paused and hummed. "Two days. One for me and one for you."

"Can you go first?" Caleb blurted. "I'm scared."

Janice looked up. Her eyes narrowed as she shook her head, then her expression softened. "Fine. You have to back me up, though."

Caleb gave her a thumbs up and laughed, which did little to calm her nerves.

The next day, the whole school was frantic. The dance was so close, and the last-minute stragglers rushed to find partners. Janice barely had the nerve to get out of class, let alone make it to the football field. With some help from Caleb, she stumbled to the bleachers, unable to push herself any further. Her wingman made the rest of the journey for her, pulling Brody off the field for a moment.

When the two boys returned, Janice jumped to her feet. "H-hey, Brody."

"Hey, Janice. Are you watching us practice?"

"I... uh, yeah. Totally down to watch you play. Guys—I mean—watch you guys..." She added a forced laugh to seal the deal.

Caleb shook his head. "Okay, this isn't what she's here for. She couldn't care less about sports. She has a question for you, right?" He not too subtly nudged her, but she stood still. She blankly stared at Brody, who tilted his head and shrugged.

"Yeah I—Oh would you look at the time." She glanced down at her nonexistent watch. "It's time for me to hit the road. Nice chatting with you. See you never." She made a one-eighty as she walked away from the boys, only for Caleb to wrangle her back. Brody watched as Caleb fruitlessly pulled at her sleeve as she wiggled her way out of his grasp. Finally, after a few shouts and friendly tugs, Janice walked right back to the bleachers.

"Brody," she shouted.

He looked back at her. "Never thought I'd see you so nervous. Not even in debate."

"Sh-shut up. Just listen. So...you—me—dance?"

The air was still. The world went silent. Janice stopped breathing, her anticipation bubbling over. Brody looked at Janice, "Oh, kind of caught me off guard. But... sure."

An eruption of cheers exploded from Caleb as he jumped around and punched the air. He dove in and pulled his two friends into one enormous bear hug. He continued to shout and holler right into their ears, too hyped up to even notice their annoyed looks.

"But I thought you and Caleb had a thing going on? I would've asked you out sooner."

"What made you think that? Wait—is it Board Game Club?"

"Yeah, it was. The rumors from literally everyone didn't help either. Could you blame me?"

Janice slapped her forehead as she shook her head. "Just promise you won't bail on our date and we can keep this up."

By the time the living noise maker calmed down, Caleb shoved Brody back onto the football field, leaving the two friends all alone. They hugged and cheered to themselves as they left the school to spend the rest of their day elsewhere.

The day after was full of panic as every few minutes, Caleb remembered his ordeal. His day would be going fine until his memory made him worry all over again. He wasn't the type to panic, but his years spent with his worrywart friend had finally rubbed off on him. Janice pried him out of his slump and slapped his back encouragingly.

"It's going to be fine. Just like you said, Mr. Confident." She smiled along as the two traversed the halls, their footsteps echoed in unison. She tugged his arm to the Book Club door. On the count of three, they swung open the door and looked inside, scanning the area for violet glasses. Once they'd found her, they beckoned Marilyn away from the novel in her lap and pulled her into the halls, the book gripped in her hands.

"W-What the heck is happening?" She nearly lost balance as Janice held her by the shoulders.

"Let's cut to the chase." Janice pointed a thumb at her best friend. "He might explode if we take too long." She then slapped Caleb's back. "Take it away, big guy."

Caleb looked like a deer in headlights, giving her a toothy grin as the hamster in his brain ran circles. "Hey, buddy." He snapped his fingers and pointed at her.

She brought the book up to her face, growing red by the second. "Hi, Caleb."

The cogs in his brain chugged along as he spoke, "So I don't know you and you don't know me, but I think it'd be great if we changed that. Maybe we can be bros? Or like, mega bros. Friends? No wait, that's not—special friends?" He turned around. "What's the word?"

Janice scoffed. "Caleb, you've been speaking English for all your life." She stepped closer to him and whispered, "We talked about this, don't fail me now."

"I'm trying, I'm trying," he shouted right back, echoing down the hall. Janice opened her mouth to retort only to be interrupted by a low chuckle from behind them. The two looked back at Marilyn, barely hiding her amusement from the whole scenario.

She slowly slipped off her glasses. "I think I know what you're trying to say." A glint shimmered in her eye as she pulled the book away from her face, revealing the smirk sitting on her face. "Caleb."

He gulped, "Yeah?"

"Let me put it in layman's terms. You wanted to ask me out because that's tradition, but you can't quite get the words out. Right?"

Caleb nodded.

"Ok, so would you want me to do the honors?"

He nodded again.

"Right so, here we go." She cleared her throat and got down on one knee, "Caleb, will you go to the dance with me?"

He took a moment to process what he was hearing before squealing, "I do."

"Now that wasn't so hard. Say something like that next time, okay?" She held his hand and brought it up to her lips. "See you tomorrow, Prince Charming." She gave it a quick peck before running off into her club room again. He stood there in silence as Janice patted his back.

"Janice, what's the word for the stinging in your chest?"

"That, my friend, is what we in the business call a crush. I think we found your type. Congratulations."

"Yeah, girls who word good."

She rolled her eyes, "I'll buy you a dictionary for your birthday. But for now," she stepped closer to him, "Shall we celebrate?"

"Aw, don't even ask me. Of course we're celebrating. Frozen yogurt, my treat."

They ran over to their local dessert shop in a heartbeat, their veins flowing with adrenaline and excitement. They couldn't hold back their giggles while they ran down the street. When they sat with frozen yogurt cups in hand, they finally had time to slow down and relax. The past forty eight hours brought up a lot of stress, but it was all worth it in their minds. Now that both of them had someone to go with, they could be at the same dance together without having to be "together."

"Finally, I can breathe again. I've been so scared all day." He scooped himself a spoonful of vanilla yogurt, cold enough to hurt his cheeks.

Janice did the same. "I know right, but we managed pretty alright." She shook as the chill hit her.

"Man, if it weren't for you I would've looked like a complete dork. And I would've never met Marilyn, so thanks bud."

"Zip it. It's only fair since you helped me out with Brody." She sighed. "Seriously, imagine running away from your crush. I was so close to just bailing after that first attempt."

Caleb smiled. "Well, I couldn't just sit around and watch my friend fall apart. It's just not like you."

"And I would never let you friend zone someone in point three seconds. Would've been hilarious, but I need someone to talk to during the dance. Speaking of which, we need outfits. I don't know about you, but the fanciest thing I own is cowboy boots."

He shook his head, "Don't worry, I'm pretty sure my mom has something your size. She's probably down to let you borrow them."

"Really? That's so sweet of you. You'd do that for me?"

"Well, we can't go if we don't wear our Sunday best. Then we wouldn't match and then my whole game would be off. What else would we be?"

She laughed and rested her head on her hand. "Best friends."

IF ONLY

by Michelle Nguyen

If only I had what you had:
A pair of spiffing legs,
A breathing soul.

If only I had what you had:
Freedom to love who I yearn for,
Freedom to be whoever I choose to be.

Only then will I be able to touch him
Without the weight of my being holding me down,
Without the fear of abandoning my identity.

Instead, I peek at him behind the mountainous rocks,
Afraid to reveal myself,
Afraid he won't see me as anything more than a foreign creature.

There he is.
His hyacinth-blue eyes fill me with elation,
Anticipation consumes my mind.

Out comes a mysterious figure.
She is the same as him,
Her eyes are also filled with life.

She is as gorgeous as the gods
With a pair of spiffing legs,
While her laughter revealed a breathing soul.

They interlock hands,
Hold each other close, and
Stroll down the sandy path.

An indescribable pain hits me.
Like a tidal wave,
It pulls me back to the ocean.

My eyes feel as though they are being scorched,
But no matter how hard I try to let the feeling go,
The fire remains.

I glance back at his dorsal.
Taking a final leap into the place I belong,
I promise to never let myself love again.

LOST DREAMS

by Michelle Nguyen

I sit still, pondering whether or not it will arrive,
My mind spins as if on a rollercoaster ride.
Is this connection worth the nosedive?
The thought of having you keeps me holding on,
But the clock ceaselessly mocks me,
Hours turn into days, days turn into months
The idea of us becomes clouded
And eventually fades
Like a dying flame.

RAINY DAYS

by Bryce Le

"It's a lovely day for rain," you said to me
With a soft smile on your face
As you gazed out the window
At the water running down the streets.

I suppose every day was a lovely day
When we were together
Protecting each other
From the world that was so unkind.

The time we spent together
Was such a small form of happiness,
But the warmth that we shared
Was just enough for us.

If you were here with me today,
You would tell me again
How lovely of a day it is
With a soft smile on your face.

You'd grab me by the arm
And pull me outside
To face the world together
With our heads held high.

But you're not here
And the ghost of your smile
Is all that remains
Of the memories we once shared.

It's a terrible day for rain.

MOTIVATION MAKES A BETTER YOU

by Marcello Juarez

Accept yourself for who you are.
Be who you want to be and ignore judgment.
Change the world and make it a better place.
Don't let others bring you down.
Embrace who you really are.
Focus on your goals.
Goals are meant to be achieved.
Have confidence in yourself.
Imagine a better you.
Justify the things you've done.
Keep on trying when things get tough.
Learn to be a better you.
Make yourself and others proud.
No matter what, always try your best.
Overcome all the obstacles you face.
Proudly express yourself.
Quitting is not an option.
Remember to try your best.
See a better future for yourself.
Trust yourself and others.
Until you achieve your goals, keep trying.
Visualize your goals, how would you achieve them?
Work your absolute best.
Xceed others' expectations and set your own.
You can achieve anything if you try hard enough.
Zero room for errors is a lie; you're allowed to make mistakes.

THE NIGHT SKY

by Marcello Juarez

Through a telescope, the night sky becomes much more.
Its tiny stars enlarge and become alive,
And the moon's details shine clearer.
Through a telescope, the night sky gains a new beauty.
The stars and moon create a speechless sight,
And the longer you stare, the more you're mesmerized.
Through a telescope, the night sky fosters curiosity.
You question the infinite possibilities of the universe,
Are we alone in this universe?
Is there life out there like us?
It seems like a simple question,
Yet the answer is harder than we think.

TETRIS

by Terry Nguyen

We're getting pushed down
And it's insane
To you, this is all a game

You're locked out of my thoughts
And I'm blocked out of yours
Left me alone, needing more

Block here, block there
How many times are you gonna block me
Now you just don't care

You're dropping me
Dropping free
But don't forget our story

You carry all the hate
That holds you down like deadweight
And you've seen it too late

Did I need you or did you need me
'Cause there's a fine line
So you decide

In my eyes, there was a compromise
But to you, that compromise was a lie
Something that couldn't be defined

Now I'm alone, left sundered
In these rains
But nah, there's thunder

And you're back saying we had a bond
Damn
Sorry, but I've moved on

You told me to let it go
But how could I let this
When our relationship's fallin' like Tetris

A LOVE LETTER

by Vivien Nguyen

A GIRL WITH BRAIDED pigtails walked through the corridor and adjusted her circle-rimmed glasses. She turned and saw a group of girls.

"So. You got the top score in class, huh?" They giggled.

"Congrats," another sneered.

"I, uh," the girl with glasses said, looking toward her shoes. "Thanks, but I have to go." She stepped right, but the trio moved in front of her. "Can you please let me through?"

"What? So we're not smart enough to talk to you?"

"That's not it—"

"I'll have you know, my parents and grandparents and great grandparents got to the top here, too." The leader stepped closer, forcing the girl to take a step back with her shaking legs. "Compared to me, you have nothing."

The girl tripped with another step back and could only mutter soft apologies before a handsome boy appeared and stood in front of her. "Would you three please stop bothering her?"

The three girls fell silent. The leader batted her eyelashes and pulled the boy away by the arm. "We're not bothering anyone."

"Yeah, it's just a little friendly teasing." One of the other girls squeezed his arm. "Hey, why don't you come to our party this weekend?"

"Sorry, but I'll have to decline." The boy said, shaking their hands off.

The leader's smile turned strained. "Well, whatever. Looks like you don't know what you're missing out on." She narrowed her eyes at the glasses girl. "And you there. Don't ever talk to me again." The group turned and walked away.

"Are you alright?" He softened his voice and reached his hand towards her.

"Thank you," she said. "Sorry, I don't know your name."

"I'm Fei, just a freshman. And there's no need to thank me." He gently patted her head. "Don't let what they said get to you. All you need is confidence."

After that incident, throughout high school, Fei grew more and more popular as did his reputation of being the protector of the vulnerable.

With that all behind him, Fei went off to college. A few years later, as a senior, he was the campus prince. Everyone knew his name. All the girls wanted to be his lover. The boys wanted to be his friend. The professors loved him. He really was the perfect man—intelligent, friendly, handsome, and creative.

However, he wasn't as perfect as everyone thought, or at least he had changed.

One day, on the way to Building D, the School of Art, Fei let his true thoughts loose but kept them confined in his mind. "Gullible girls, easily falling for my charms. I have nothing but tricks and bluffs, yet they still believe me? Goes to show that confidence is everything." Two giggling underclassmen, young women with poofy blonde hair, passed by him, waving and smiling. Fei hitched his backpack higher on his right shoulder. "Obedient dogs, always following my commands. I should give them some kind of treat next time. Maybe another pat on the head?" He chuckled and looked at his watch.

Fei opened the front doors to Building D, bounded up the stairs, two at a time, and entered the large room, a well-stocked art studio. Head held high, he strode past a table group of three smiling brunettes staring, wide-eyed.

Fei picked a seat at an open table by the window facing the center of the campus. He glanced outside, making sure everyone could see him. He took out his sketchbook and gathered some art supplies from around the room: acrylic paints, paintbrushes, canvas, palette, paper towels, jar of water, and varnish. He spread everything in a half-circle around him, taking over the entire tabletop surface large enough for four students.

Throughout his college life, the art building was where Fei most often felt at home. He would become so immersed in his painting that he lost track of time.

Night began to fall and a soft touch on Fei's shoulder broke his focus. He jerked up and turned.

"Excuse me. Sorry to bother you," a girl with silver glasses said softly, her gaze shifted to the floor, "but you should get going. It's late. I think they're going to close up the building."

"Oh, thank you." Fei looked out the windows. The last light of dusk was disappearing beyond the horizon. "I should get going." Fei scrambled to gather his brushes and return the supplies to the cabinets and shelves. He shoved a sketchbook into his backpack and sauntered down the hallway and down the staircase.

Fei turned the corner and headed to his private rented studio, a single well-lit room useful for his artistic endeavors. It was nearby on a quiet street free of the noisy university distractions.

"Ah, finally," Fei said. He stood in front of the glass door, patting down his pants and looking through his pockets. "Where did I leave my keys?" He dropped his backpack to the floor.

"Excuse me." There was the soft voice again. "I'm sorry I followed you here, but you left your keys. I tried to get your attention but didn't want to scream at you."

"Oh, you're that girl. Thank you. You've helped me out so much today." Fei glanced at his surroundings. "Not many people know I come here. Shhh. Don't say anything. This is where the real masterpieces are created."

"Of course. I wouldn't think of it. I'll get going now." The girl walked back into the darkness, vanishing.

Fei finally unlocked the door and entered his studio. He set his things at his desk and gathered the rest of his supplies from under the counter storage cabinets before pulling up a stool and absorbing himself into his latest project, a grand landscape complete with rolling hills and a meadow surrounded by trees. He dabbed his fan brush into green and yellow paint and dabbed at the canvas.

A knock sounded from the door. Fei glanced out the large floor to ceiling window, now black with night, only reflecting back his own image. "Who would come here at this hour?" He squinted at the glass. A few slivers of moonlight pouring from the sky streamed through the panes.

Knock, knock.

The sound grew louder.

Knock, knock.

And louder.

Knock. Knock.

"Who is it?" Fei called, still flicking brushstrokes of paint on his project.

Knock. Knock.

Fei raised his voice. "Could you stop with the knocking?" Though the knocking didn't stop. In fact, it continued louder and more rapid than before.

Knock. Knock. Knock.

"Fine." Fei pushed himself up. "I'm coming." He approached the door, but the knocking immediately halted.

All that could be heard was the sound of the breeze and the crickets. Fei faced the front door, but his hand stopped—as if his subconscious told him not to open it. Staring at the door, he felt something, a strange feeling, an aura, that he couldn't describe. He stepped back.

Silence.

Fei stood there for what felt like forever, frozen as his mind raced, wondering what could be behind the door. The knocking could have been caused by many things…. Maybe a branch tapping in the wind, or a small animal lost and trying to get in. It could have been anything.

Fei let out a soft, reassuring laugh.

Knock knock knock knock knock.

Fei jolted backward. He hesitated in his approach to the door, one foot at a time. Right. Left. Right. Left.

His instinct was warning him, but warning him about what?

He had nothing to fear. He was better than fear. He was untouchable.

With each closing step, the banging grew louder and louder. From only a foot away from the door, Fei should've been able to see a silhouette through the fogged glass, yet he saw no such thing. No one was outside, but the knocking persisted.

It was nothing more than an annoyance invading his concentration. He had a painting to finish.

Or maybe it was more than a benign annoyance.

Fei took deep breaths. In and out, in and out. He stalled for one last second before taking the final step.

Knock knock knock.

But nothing was there outside the glass door. He could see the streetlights in the distance. Maybe he hadn't been getting enough sleep lately. Or too much coffee.

Or not enough.

Sweat dripped down the side of his face, his breathing grew ragged, his hands shook. With his eyes focused on the glass door, he reached for the lock on the doorknob.

Knock knock knock.

With that set of knocks, Fei felt something run throughout his body, something cold and smooth. His thumb and index finger pinched the lock. Slow twist, then a click, and then silence. His hand wrapped around the knob and turned, but before he could open the door, something fluttered down and landed on the doorstep.

It wasn't loud. In fact, it was barely audible. Fei turned his gaze down to find a letter on the ground. He unlocked the door and bent down. With nimble hands, he picked up the letter, flipping it back and forth. The envelope was small, only about the size of his palm. It had an ivory white color, yet thin enough for the pink undertone of the letter to seep through.

He peered to the right and left. The street was empty as were the sidewalks. There was a wind rustling through the leaves and the crickets had resumed their chirping.

He realized the knocking had stopped and with it, the strange aura disappeared, but he was still trembling. The source of his restlessness hadn't disappeared. It only shifted to the letter in his hand.

Fei returned to and laid the letter on his desk. Receiving letters was nothing new to him, but there was one fact that caused his shivering: no one should have known about his studio. He never received letters at his studio.

Fei clenched the envelope and slid a spare palette knife underneath the flap. He took a deep breath and pushed the blade, cleanly cutting the envelope. Fei pulled out the pink paper and read the words written in red:

Dear Fei, My Eternal Love,

Words cannot describe how I feel about you. The Romeo to my Juliet, you are the moon to my night sky. The cool water to my burning fire, you are untouchable. And for that, I admire and love you.

Oh, I remember the first time we met. It was the beginning of a new semester and I was a new transfer student. I had a tough time fitting in, and all the girls would tease me about the way I looked. Calling me a "nobody" because of my braided hair and large circle rimmed glasses. We only spoke briefly, when you saved me from the bullies, but the time we spent together meant everything to me. I fell in love.

I waited for you every day, at the same spot, at the same time. You would rarely come, but each time you did, even when no words were exchanged, I gained a new moment to treasure. I couldn't hold my desire for you, so I followed you around these last couple years. I enrolled in the same college, chose the same major. I learned of your schedule. In the morning, seven sharp, I would wait for you by the entrance of the campus. Seeing you get out of your car was the start of my day. When you got hungry you would always eat the same snack, chocolate. You try so hard to hide your sweet tooth cravings that I fell deeper in love with you. Then to end my day I would watch you from afar as you painted until night at your secret studio.

However, it hurt when I saw you with other women. My blood boiled. They didn't know you like I did. They shouldn't have been the ones you were talking to. You should have been talking to me.

I know of your secret. One that would ruin the reputation you cherish so much. Although you may hate me if you find out, I will still love you no matter what. And perhaps, you'll thank me. I will be waiting at the same spot and time we usually meet.

With Undying Love,
The Love of Your Life

Is this some kind of joke? This can't be true.

"Waiting at the same spot we usually meet?" he asked aloud.

No response.

The ominous silence drove fear into Fei. His throat tightened. He ripped the letter into bits and pieces, crumpling them into a ball.

"Who could it be?" He threw the destroyed letter across the room. "I've been kind. I've been keeping my reputation as polished as possible. I'm everyone's 'prince.' No one challenges me. What could I have done wrong?" he said. Again, nothing but the crickets outside responded.

The sender knew Fei, but what did she really know?

Why me? Why me? "Why—"

"Because it's you." A soft voice passed through Fei's ears.

That girl. The one from the art classroom. The one with his keys.

"You... show yourself. Where are you? What do you want from me? What do you know?"

The soft voice giggled.

"I'll find you... Once I do, you're dead," he said. "You'll never be able to hide from me. You hear me? You'll pay for coming here."

"Fei, you can stop bluffing. You know you can't hurt me. You love me too much."

"No. You don't know anything about my feelings. You don't know me."

"Won't you stop fighting it? I'm the only one who can give everything you deserve."

"I've already told you. No." Fei looked around, trying to find where the voice was coming from, but in vain.

117

"How dare you. When this is my only chance at happiness. When I've done so much work to gather up the confidence and finally confess."

"I'm sorry, but I can't—I don't even *know* you."

"Oh well. If you can't accept me, then I'll just make sure you can never forget me."

Weeks went by and there was no word from Fei.

One early evening, the landlord, an older woman in a long, flowery dress, approached the door.

"Fei?" she called out. "You haven't paid your rent and you're not answering my calls." She knocked on the door. "I phoned your parents. They're worried and asked me to come check on you. You haven't been in school." She inserted keys in the door and twisted open the lock, but it was already unlocked. "I'm coming in." The door swung open. "Goodness, you need to remember to lock your door. What would happen if someone barged in?"

The woman shrieked.

The room was a pitch black. Lights off, windows covered. A stench permeated the room.

A voice giggled. "Knock knock…"

"Fei?"

"No, it's his Juliet."

A girl with braids, wearing metal-rimmed glasses sat calmly at the studio table, paintbrush in hand. She was painting the canvas red.

Blood red.

When What You Have is Enough

by Julia Do

It takes a certain kind of courage to tell
    your children that the world is not their own:

When you have sacrificed your eldest,
    laid bare your crimes and Crème de La Mer,

Surrendered your pressed jasmine and love
    poems, swallowed gold and truth and foreign tongues—

When you have left no daughters to wander about or to spit upon
    your grave and no ghosts with whom to make amends—

When you have lit the last stem of incense, set the
    last altar, boiled the last kettle of chrysanthemum tea—

You have anointed your body with the sins
    of your father and promised yourself to some great-grandchild—

And you have kissed the faces of ten generations—
    over and over again.

NEVER ALONE

by Vy Ngo

I remember the moment
when his heart stopped beating
My innocence lost—
I knew he'd never come back
I remember his eyes, peaceful with regret
I remember him in a dream
He took me on his bike,
We fell and I saw him, in the distance
A white outfit under a black sky
He looked at me and then walked away
Was that a goodbye?
I was on my own and felt alone
On a dark, lonely road
I've been on it for quite some time
Where was I going? Where will I go?

The Old Man put his foot forth and stopped me
His light radiates in this dark space
With gray hair, wisdom wearing him down
Tell me, Old Man, what was your road?
Was it as lonely as mine?
"It's been a long way," he said.
The Old Man, will I see him again?
The warmth from your Light,
It reminds me of him
I remember, now, I remember
Old Man, this lonely road,
Where do you fit in?
Our paths will never collide,
But somehow you're here

You're here, in this long piece of road
It's been quite a long time
You stepped onto this road
Your light spreading throughout this space
The path isn't clear, yet
But your light is comforting
"Don't be scared," he said.
Further down the road,
I know I'll lose that Light
But Old Man, you'll always be here.
I can't look back, and I have to let you go
But for now, I'll hold on to that light.
Thank you, Old Man, for I was never alone.

DECK OF CARDS

by Kathleen Vu

Oh? You want to hear my story?
I am trapped, cramped in a tight space.
With only one door, we leave as a unit,
A society of similar faces arranged in specific groups.

This "shelter" is supposed to protect us all
From harm, danger, and foreign elements.
Yet do You know what I see?

A single-cell prison of cardboard walls
While big enough for 54, maybe more,
I can't breathe.

Even without this prison,
Society wraps us tightly together with
A rubber band of laws and assumptions.

To break free,
I must fight every presumption
But suffer as an outcast.
To sit still,
I must silently follow the social construct
But suffer mental and emotional pain.

You think Life is nothing but a game.
When I leave the "shelter,"
I am forced to play by Your rules.

There's no personal space,
No room to breathe, but here I am,
A pawn—no—

A card in Your hand,
And I've had enough.
How can I follow Your rules if I can't be like You?

I'm done living a lie,
I'm done telling myself lies.
Unlike You,
My heart beats for nobody.

Who am I?
What am I?
I am an ace
And finally
Free.

UNCULTURED

by Mariana Escalona Diaz

But mother I don't want to go
Wish not to put on a pretty bow
Bow my head in submission
I ask for permission
To speak my mind but you say no.

Chin up, stand tall, shoulders back
Try not to think of what you lack
You will be reminded, but laugh it off
Don't you dare be bold and scoff
At the rules kept neat in a stack

Enough. No more.
I now hold my head up high and
Make up my own rules
As they call me defiant and troublesome,
I nod and smile,

I am happier speaking my mind.

THE AMERICAN DREAM
by Mariana Escalona Diaz

How can I strive for better
When I lack the fundamentals?
A rug of hope pulled out from under me
And like a baby, I begin to crawl.
A shred of hope in the distance,
The light at the end of the tunnel, dimmed.
Not gone, but fading.
My heart is torn at defeat of morality.

Working towards something,
Millions of dreams at hand.
I've faced insomnia
Only to forget to live dreams as my reality.
Whenever I sleep, I blackout.
My touch with my fantasies is no longer
Than the lifespan of a doll at a child's careless hands.

I was promised a better future,
The ability to dream beyond the unknown.
Stripped of my rights,
Left-handed without the ability to write.
Trapped inside a room with
The walls caving in.
At the border lies an illusion,
Alienation from society worsens.
Distinctions between you and me more prominent.
What does it mean to be free?

RED MOUNTAIN TRAIL

by Shannon Le

IT WAS LUNCH BREAK at the cafe when the red threads appeared around Daniel's finger.

He tuned out his coworkers' chatter and looked towards the table, where his hand rested. At first the string was as long as an earthworm coiling around his pinky. When it made a firm knot that pressed into his skin, the frayed ends twisted inch by inch into a uniform string, climbing upwards. He followed the spinning thread until the loose end disappeared into low clouds.

"Did you see that?" Daniel interrupted their conversation, his eyes still pointed toward the sky.

"See what?" Sam, the portly guy, turned around in his chair.

The blonde woman, Corey or Laurie, Daniel couldn't quite remember, looked up too. "It's just the airshows, nothing special."

"No, not the airshow. It's right there," he said, pointing at the string. "Keep looking."

Corey-Laurie squinted. "There's nothing there."

"Oh, I get it." A smile cracked on Sam's face as he crossed his arms. "You're doing another bit."

Daniel leaned back in his seat and admitted defeat. "Yeah." He put his hands up while forcing a laugh. "You got me."

"Thought so." Corey-Laurie sighed. "Thanks for not taking yourself too seriously. It's refreshing when everyone here is so hard-nosed."

"Have you looked at me?" Daniel asked with a smirk. "Can't really take myself too seriously as a gangly ginger."

The two of them chuckled, and soon Daniel followed along reluctantly. He'd hoped that people would see him as a respectable adult once in a while, but maybe no matter what he accomplished or how he worked, he wouldn't even the playing field after all. Maybe he was only there to make others feel better about themselves. At least it was better than being alone. Right?

Soon, one of their watches sounded, and Daniel returned to the uncomfortable silence of his desk. His reports, his computer screen, his third cup of coffee, everything was a blur except for the bright red string. What kind of person was attached to the other end beyond the clouds? A pilot? An astronaut? A guardian angel? Maybe a person wasn't at the other end at all, and he was only destined for a cardboard box. It didn't matter, so long as he had something to do instead of sitting around in one place; Daniel knew that he wouldn't be able to stop the tapping of his foot and the twirl of his pen until he went and found out.

He got up and slung his backpack over his shoulder. Once he left the office space and entered the hallway, he approached the supervisor's desk. "Jeff, I'm clocking out early today."

The older man met him with a glare. "All right. But be careful about not pulling your weight, rookie."

"Of course," Daniel said, controlling the irritation that crept into his voice. Jeff would probably call Daniel "rookie" this year, the year after that, and five decades after that, if he was still around. Sure, people said he treated everyone like that, but Daniel could never be sure.

"Aw, they'll be fine. We have the best team in town."

"Hmm, really? When they've recruited you?" Jeff said. "Could you tell me the reason?"

Much too late, the realization hit Daniel. There was no way he could convince the supervisor by talking about a psychic string. He had never been one to think things through and found himself in trouble because of it. "Just some family business."

He raised an eyebrow before grumbling, "Surely it could wait a few hours. It's already a Friday."

"It's no crime to let me have some privacy, right?"

Daniel could see the supervisor's look of contempt. "All right." He wrote something down with a loud scratch of his pen. Just as Daniel walked through the door, he heard the older man add, "And talk to me, Monday at eight A.M. sharp, to make up your hours."

"All right." Daniel waved quickly with his back turned, and rushed to his car.

Even in his tiny apartment, Daniel had made space for camping gear and a pair of hiking boots, used exactly once on a family trip. He never quite got over his childhood obsession with survival TV shows, even now that he knew they were staged. He still loved the idea of living off the land. With a thud, Daniel tossed his gear into the trunk of his car and settled into the driver's seat. Nothing but the thrill of adventure propelled him as he drove headlong towards the thread's direction.

An hour later, a sign that read "King's Crown Trailhead" came into view. Pines and spruces sprung up around him as he drove along the string's path. After a quick hello to the ranger, Daniel drove through the gate and parked next to jeeps and vans by wooden cabins.

Soon he was alone on the trail, feet on gravel, nose drying at the tip from the wind. He swallowed and took a deep breath as if about to plunge into the ocean. Maybe he would walk for a little along the string then turn back, he thought. He settled on that for a few hours as he took the winding trail ahead of him.

Pine trees appeared as he continued up the trail. Daniel's eyes widened as the red string snaked into the dense green needles. Did he have to go there? Those stories of dead hikers mauled by bears or ghosts or ghost bears flashed through Daniel's head. His legs trembled in his boots as a sick feeling crept into his stomach. If there was any time to turn back, it was now.

He took a deep breath to calm his mind. It was a noble thing to risk it all for a soulmate, after all. Daniel parted the dense leaves with a swipe of his arms and followed the string.

Spots of sunlight shone through the treetops as the leaves crunched under his boots. The fresh smell of evergreens and crisp air relieved him a little.

"This isn't so bad."

He wouldn't die. Every step was one step closer to his fate.

The sun glared when he left the shroud of trees, and Daniel shielded his eyes. Daniel's red thread shot up onto the gray-and-white flecked stone. He had hiked before, but the jagged boulders and rough terrain seemed like something only a mountain goat could climb. Still, it was possible. His soulmate had done it. Probably many times too, if the string disappeared into the stratosphere on a weekday.

After hours of stumbling through the rocks, Daniel finally found a steady rhythm. The peak was fast approaching, and the red line ended just a little outside of sight. Daniel's face had turned red and dry from the wind, but that didn't matter when he was so close. He had just a little more to go, just one step after the other.

He figured that he earned a break. As he sat at the foot of a spruce tree to rest his feet, silence settled all around him. It seemed too high an altitude for anything but dry shrubs, or eagles surveying the skies for prey.

Then the ground rumbled. He bolted to his feet. Boulders tumbled down the slope towards him. He ran, his boots slipping on wet leaves as he struggled not to fall. His breath became ragged.

The boulders finally rolled to the foot of the mountain. Daniel looked around in circles, with no clue as to where he was.

He heard something and prayed he heard wrong. Droplets of rain splattered on the ground, and the light of the day slowly faded. Daniel turned tail once again, pulling his hood over his head. There was a small cave opening in front of him. Ducking down with a scrunched neck, he stumbled into the darkness of the cave and left the curtain of rain behind him.

He crouched, sinking into his jacket and resting his face on his knees. Though it wasn't the best place to hide from the rain, and a few drops fell onto the edge of his coat, he didn't dare move farther from the dim circle of light coming through a gap in the wall. A little cold was nothing compared to the unknown terrors that lay deeper in the cave's darkness.

The red string mocked him with its stubborn glow among the gloom around it. This was what he got for straying from the beaten path. Did he have any common sense at all, rushing up here so late with no plan to get down? Daniel dug out a squashed bologna sandwich from his backpack and chewed miserably.

He had no idea how long he had sat. Then a light voice interrupted the drizzle of rain. "Hello?"

Daniel looked back outside the cave. Nothing but a sprinkle. He looked behind him. Just rock. He stood up and brushed off the dust from his legs, looking down. More rock.

"Above you." A gloved hand reached through the gap over his head. "I'll pull you up."

"Are you sure?"

"It'll be fine. Trust me." Daniel gripped the hand as tightly as he could, and its owner took another hand to pull him up by the rest of his arm. Once he was out of the cave, the sky had turned orange and red.

"What are you doing here?" his rescuer asked. She wore her black hair in a practical braid, and stood unusually tall, near his height. And, just a few inches from him, the hundred-mile string finally ended at her hand.

He could hardly contain his excitement. For all he knew, he was still the only one who could see the string. "Just looking for something. Are you here to find something too?"

"Hmm? Not at all." Her dark eyes stayed fixed, and she took no notice of his hand. "I needed some fresh air, after being in the observatory all day."

"The observatory?" So much for rushing into this place without reading up on it.

"That's probably what you're looking for. Just follow me, I'll show you the way."

"Nah, I shouldn't. I should try and turn back home before it's too dark."

"At this hour, your odds of going back alone in one piece aren't good." She raised her hand to her chin. "You can stay up there for the night, until a shuttle bus takes you down in the morning. Besides, you get to see the best part."

"And what's that?" he asked.

A smile crept over her placid face. "You'll get there right when the stars come out."

Daniel smiled back. "Thanks," he said. "You're going through some trouble for me."

She became unreadable again. "Don't mention it. It's not every day I find somebody inside a hole in the ground."

He laughed the truest laugh he had all day. "That's amazing. You said that with such a straight face." He saw a hint of her smile again and winded down. "By the way, I'm Daniel," he said, reaching his hand out, red string still attached. He couldn't reveal it just yet. Best to allow her to make her own decision. All he asked for in that moment was to be connected.

She accepted his hand. "Call me Nora."

The moment their hands connected, the red string glowed.

ROLLING TANGERINE
by Christine Vu

My tangerine fell and rolled away
Down a tall hill and shouted hurray
"At last, I can be free!"
On its escaping spree,
Before it plopped down into a bay

TRUTH & LIES
by Christine Vu

Truth
Candid, Point-Blank
Opening, Assuring, Guaranteeing
Verity, Authenticity, Fabrication, Trickery
Covering, Fibbing, Deceiving
Mendacious, Underhanded
Lies

FOR HER

by Julie Tran

Thump, thump, thump
I feel as though the crowd can hear my heartbeat,
Thump, thump, thump,
Today will be the one day I cannot accept defeat.

Three more minutes until the race of my life,
Three more minutes of everything I've worked for
Until it all comes to light
Until I decide to open or close the door

"Don't be afraid,"
My mother's voice echoes in the distance
"All of your hard work was man-made."
Her presence, the foundation of my existence.

The horn roars and I dive off
My face hits the water and I don't stop.
I can't stop, I know all of this will pay off
One more minute of pain, for a lifetime of being on top.

The tiredness and pain stab like a blade,
Yet, in a way, I want to stay in this moment forever,
Then I remember my mother's voice, "Don't be afraid."
I touch the wall and look up to the crowd, my supporters.

In that moment, I know.
I am not just fighting for me,
I am fighting for her, too.

I thank her for being her.
for being my shelter
For loving me when I don't
For everything,
For being my Mom.

DAWN

by Brian Ly

First sight of day's light
The rays spread across the land
To life, the world wakes

DAY

by Brian Ly

Pitter and patter
The lands work from end to end
For life, we harvest

DUSK

by Brian Ly

Soleil has fallen
Her kingdom shines no longer
To rest, we follow

NIGHT

by Brian Ly

Under Luna's watch
Darkness covers the ruins
For rest, we're silent

TENDRILS

by Alexa Wright

Based on graphic art Name: Non-conservative Forces of an
Imaginary Pendulum.

Artist: Alexa Wright
Created using a program the author made on Python.

Into the heart of recursion
Endless tendrils reaching
Grasping at a chance to converge
To be accompanied by one another

How lonely they must be
With the intent to stretch infinitely
Bound by the unknown
A fickle finite cage

Infinitesimal in scale and infinite in scope
How unfathomable it must be
To be a finite tendril
In an endless world

They know not what they reach for
A point shrouded in mystery
They cannot see the principles
That drive them to converge

I am a tendril
I know not where I'll go
I reach with foolish fervor
To an end that is unknown

FINALS AT LA QUINTA

by Alexa Wright

There once was a lousy student
Who liked to think himself prudent
As finals draw near
He shed not a tear
As he was both dumb and impudent.

THE ROSE

by Kady Tran

Pink, yellow and red,
I wish it wasn't all in my head.

The life I wanted, the life I chose,
All depended on that rose.

As I sat here in silence with him,
I just remembered all of his sins.

"Are you really the one for me?"
Well, you're not exactly what I need.

The sun was sinking and so was my heart,
I took a deep breath as it turned dark.

"Tomorrow I choose my bachelorette."
"But if it's not you, please, don't fret."

I rolled my eyes.
But continued staring at the sky.

Blue, yellow and black.
I already knew you and I could never last.

You enjoyed the morning,
I enjoyed the night,
I could not stand having you in my sight.

So tomorrow, it better not be me,
Or else it'll be the last day that you will ever see.

SHE'S SO PERFECT

by Kady Tran

Everyone says that she's so perfect,
But they've never seen what I've seen
Under the light of the moon,
millions of stars illuminating her,
All I saw was sadness.
Strange how someone who seemed so perfect,
So whole,
Could be so shattered.

Everyone says that she's so perfect.
But as our fingertips touched,
All I could feel was her ice-cold skin.
Despite the fire dancing in front of our eyes,
She sent shivers down my spine.

How could an angel so perfect like her fall?

FACE IT

by Keanu Hua

"WHAT DO YOU MEAN you can't produce anything better than this, Curt?"

"Gods, sir, I'm sorry, I'm so, so sorry—"

"Get out." I barely had time to run before a chair crashed against the door.

But that was weeks ago, when I used to be an artist for a game company, back when I could make something pretty for other people even if my boss was a total jerk. But now I had nothing, and I couldn't see myself getting a new job for a few weeks at least.

So, I figured that I'd have to go and talk with my landlord about the rent. Maybe he could cut me a break for at least a month. Joseph was a strange guy—I'd never seen his door open, heard a toilet flush, or seen anything in front of his office door on the first floor. It was like he didn't even exist, but I was sure he had to, because I always heard something on the other side when I turned in my rent, slipping the envelope underneath the door.

But when I got to his door, there was a note: "In the garden. Be back soon."

That's weird. I had never seen a note there before, and I hadn't been out to the apartment garden since moving in a couple years ago. Guess it was time to explore.

I walked out back into the garden. Well, a garden is understating it—it was more or less a jungle, filled with ferns and trees and bushes. Funny I hadn't noticed it before. Must've been too busy with work.

For the main parts of the garden, I could see rubber trees, coffee plants, and orchids, among others, but those three were the most common. Other than them, there was the dense canopy made up of overgrown iron pergolas and trees bent over to provide shade, and some streams leading into small ponds. There was a cat by one of them, looking at the water, but when I came near, it ran.

After I finish with my landlord, I'm going to have to come back and draw this place. Maybe that art piece can land me another job.

I paused at a concrete bench. Before I get lost in this place looking for the guy, I could at least relax a little. I sat down at an arbor surrounded by rubber trees.

This place was fantastic. I must've looked weird forming a rectangle with my hands and turning around, trying to find the perfect spot to draw.

But one thing caught my eye. A rubber tree stood deep and concealed in the brush.

It had these knotholes and some curves in the bark, making it look like a face—two big eyes, exhausted, like me, and a mouth frowning way, way too much, like someone stretched out a person's mouth while they were screaming. Plus, there was a knife stuck out of it like a toothpick. Sitting there, staring at it, I swear, it was watching me, a baleful gaze from the darkness. For a moment, I wanted to draw it, but then its face moved. Smiled.

I jumped right out of my seat. After I rubbed my eye, I took another look. The smile was a frown again. I was probably just seeing things. It was just stress. Yeah, that was it.

I searched the rest of the jungle in my own little expedition, imagining myself as some explorer in the African wilderness. Every little stream was a roaring river, every unidentified plant was named, and every rubber tree had a face in it. It might have been some weird native ritual, something terrifying and unknown. That's why I, the brave explorer Curt, was so nervous. But in the end, I would conquer all.

Every tree had a face, though, so that bold claim seemed doubtful. They looked like people frozen in agony, and it just made me so uncomfortable, because somehow, I felt like I was staring at a mirror to myself. And besides, I could've sworn I saw that one move...

As for my landlord, he wasn't in the garden at all. I did find some gardening tools that got left behind in a hurry, a trowel, rake, and some gloves.

I left and went back to the landlord's door. I knocked. "Hey, Joseph."

There was some shuffling inside. "Yes?"

"I got fired from my job earlier today, so I was wondering if there was any way possible if you let me hold off on the rent for a month or two. I could make it up later, but I really just don't have the cash to pay you this month and—"

"Really now?" his voice called out from the other sound of the closed door. I was talking to a piece of wood. "Well, in that case, we'll find some other way to pay. Just don't worry about it for now."

"That's wonderful. Thank you so much." I turned around, but then hesitated. "And while I'm here, have you ever noticed there are faces in the rubber trees?"

"That's ridiculous. Don't be so paranoid. There aren't faces on the rubber trees. If there are any, you're just imagining them. You're probably just a little stressed. Anyone who just lost their job would be stressed, right? Why don't you go take a rest out in the garden?"

"Well, of course I'm stressed. But I don't know if I feel comfortable in the garden with the faces watching me."

"Watching you? Trust me, Curt, that place is as safe as any. You design video games, right? You've got a great imagination. Don't you do the art for all those jungle horror games? Couldn't you use a little inspiration?"

"You've got that right." I yawned. "I think I'll head back out."

"Before you go, I do believe I left my tools out there, actually. Could you perhaps go and get them? You do that while I make my preparations, Curt. See, a jungle like that needs constant care."

"Sure." The guy did just waive my rent, so it was the least I could do, even if the garden made me anxious. Besides, he was probably right. I did love my horror, so I was probably just projecting my art into my reality.

I didn't see any faces this time, but I did find his gardening tools. They felt pretty sticky. Maybe a rubber tree had dripped some latex onto it or something.

When I got back, the door to his room was open. "Hey, Joseph, I got your—"

Something cold dripped onto my shoulder. A drop of white latex oozed from the ceiling, then another, and another. "What the—" I spun around, looked up and down, trying to see where it came from, but the dripping stopped by that point. "Joseph, where are you? What was that?"

"What was what?" He spoke from behind me, with a little laugh in his voice as he covered my mouth.

For a man who spent so much time locked away, his hand was black.

Charred black. And way bigger than any human's. I shut my eyes and screamed as his hands scraped across my face and pulled at my mouth. I shook him off and scrambled outside his room.

"Tell me." Joseph crawled out of the room like a worm, his body squishing on the carpeted floor, laughing as he taunted me. "Tell me what you saw."

What happened to the landlord that I had known?

He was gigantic, barely able to fit in the tight hallway or in the doorframe, and his skin was charred black, spliced here and there and folded back in so that little pieces were dangling off of him.

I threw Joseph's gardening tools at his massive body. Latex dripped out of his wounds where they hit. His white eyes stared at me like an old wooden idol of a forgotten, wrathful god. His mouth was cut open so that his jaw hung loose from his head, tongue lashing out into the hallway. One hand landed on the floor, the other grabbed the doorframe as he wrenched himself out of the room, his latex-soaked legs soaked into the carpet.

He let go, but soon his fingers wriggled and snaked towards me, dropping pieces of ash along the way. Dozens of charred hands blossomed, crawled, wriggled out of the open wounds in his skin, eager to grasp at something.

"Come on, tell me what you saw."

I looked at the front door to the apartment complex. The way out, the only way out, was blocked by an enormous tree, cut up and bleeding rubber, among... I don't know what it was, it was like flowers were growing out of that tree. These brown flowers, with red stems snaking down the trunk.

Those were *hands* growing out of that tree.

I needed to get out—to the garden.

"Tell me, Curt, what did you see?" the creature yelled as he pursued me, latex squishing on the walls and hands groping. A few managed to grab onto my leg, but I peeled them off before I opened the garden door and shut it, leaning against it, holding it shut. He banged on it. "Open up, Curt!"

"No way."

"I swear... I swear..." His voice trailed off, and the banging stopped.

He stared at me.

And smiled, but it was more like his skin tried to peel upwards in some distortion of one.

A voice next to me spoke. "So you'll trust us then?"

"Wha—" I turned to my left, and I noticed one of the rubber trees faces talking to me.

"Dear me, you're in a sorry state, aren't you?" the face said, its teeth carved of bark chattering as they shuffled up and down. "But don't worry, you'll make it out."

I looked around. There was nothing except me, the garden, a talking tree, and the Joseph creature separated only by a thin glass door.

"How?" I asked the tree. It was like my warped games coming to life.

"Trust me, you will," another voice said to my left.

A root wrapped around my leg.

"Remember what Joseph said about payment for rent?" a third voice called out.

"What?" I looked around and rested my eyes on the talking tree to my left.

"Landlord Joseph," the face said, smiling, "I have him. Won't you come out?"

I was pulled away from the door.

The Joseph-creature pushed open the door and inched closer to me, smiling.

"Well, you won't be having to worry about rent anymore, Curt. Now, hold still..."

He tore off my hands, and I fell unconscious as tree roots snaked their way into my limbs.

When I awoke, I saw another tenant, an older woman—I think I'd seen her jogging in the mornings. My view was shielded by leaves hanging from the trees. The woman was sitting at an arbor, frowning.

"I just don't know how I'm going to pay my rent."

A PAINTER NEVER AGES

by Katherine Pham

Not old bones
Frailness or loose skin
Shakiness or cloudy eyes
Or a dweller of a soundless world.

Only youth and passion
Through a heart that will beat forever
And vision that never clouds
A young boy sits on a wooden stool.

Warped fingers paint steadily
In a world of his own making
Greying eyes see perfectly
But only when he closes them

Under closed eyes
Everything can be seen
Bugs crawling beneath blades of grass
Silhouettes dancing under a setting orange sun
Like sibling foxes frolicking in a flower field

The old man,
The young boy,
Takes one last breath
The paintbrush is set down gently
Gnarled fingertips run along the drying canvas

He has found peace within his heart.

I FELL IN LOVE IN NEW YORK

by Katherine Pham

In New York,
Homes are castles,
Glistening, soaring.
Cold to the touch, especially on
Bitter winter days and nights

Our cheeks puffed bright red,
Misty clouds of air escaped our lips
Fingers nibbled by the frost
Until they were held

"If you look at the sky,"
You said, leaning towards me
"You can see our whole future."
And as I peered up

I saw love and laughter
Two precious silver rings,
tickets to France,
a warm little home

White picket fences,
A dainty silver mailbox,
Rich cared-for grass,
And a dog in the yard

Cold nights with warm bodies,
Coffee under the rain,
Sweet candy kisses,
And a kind son

"I see that too
And I see something more,"
He whispered to me,
"Two small figures
Who had lived a good life."

MEMORY LOSS

by Mariana Escalona Diaz

We maintained eye contact
I was the first to stray
A brief moment of connection
And my heart sank,
In despair, I almost shed a tear
Asking for shelter
Hiding away
My heart aching
No point in allowing pain in
A simple glance means the world
I don't need much
For I'm a simple human
Attachment towards these memories
May cause my downfall
How can I rid myself of these
Superficial things we may toss
Yet they are etched into my mind
A sequence of images appears
As I pass a place we once shared
Rid me of the pain
Hold me close; in a whisper
Tell me that you love me
Walk away and take it all with you.

ROOM FOR GROWTH

by Mariana Escalona Diaz

A broken soul
Walks with little guidance.
The shred of hope it once had is now lost,
Many traumas, developed
There are still obstacles to overcome.
With patience and love,
Hold out your hand.
Life is not easy.
It comes with pain and is overwhelming.
But there is beauty among the pain,
Growth in the most shriveled flower.
If nurtured correctly, it will grow beautifully
The flower started off a broken soul,
But now heals its wounds with bandages.

Growth is not instant.
There are no "miracles" here.
Remember to water me.

BRIDGE

by Terry Nguyen

We were like the bridge by the pond
That people sometimes walk on

It represented our bond
Guess that's something we never thought upon

When we broke, the bridge also fell
Now I'm in pieces, shattered as well

I tried rebuilding the bridge
Before I rebuilt myself

But I stored the thought away
Like a book on a shelf

I wish you were here
But you disappeared

I'm drowned in sorrow
Our yesterday no longer has a tomorrow

The water was our end
And without the bridge I fell in

Now I'm alone, redirecting the blame
When deep inside I know you don't feel the same

I'm going insane
By myself in these rains

Maybe if I put more effort
You wouldn't have left first

But I'm selfish, in pain
In my own lane

Time I need
So much time you took

I'm in denial
It's been like that for awhile

I'm walking around the water for miles
How can I smile

Now I'm alone, down in a ridge
Thinking of our time on that bridge

YOUNG LOVE

by Benson Truong

It was as early as 4th grade,
When we first met, when we first played.
Seemed like the start of a new friendship,
but you weren't there to stay.
Then it was 8th grade.
I tried to relight the flame.
You had changed, yet stayed the same.
But our conversations became stale and short,
Meaningless, aimless, and distorted.
It was then 10th grade,
When I was given a final chance.
If I can't say anything now,
when would I advance?
Throughout the year, you had my attention.
You were blind to not see my intentions.
The fateful day came quick,
Where I faced you and had to act slick.
"You'd make a perfect first girlfriend,"
I said,
"With you, out of this world, I can transcend."
Now it is 11th grade
This time I'm not alone,
My angel came from above,
I guess you can call this
young love.

SKIPPING STONES

by Benson Truong

In the midst of the woods,
through the shady eerie night sky,
the trees open up to a lake.
Shimmering, clear, calm
Mosquitoes whine and buzz,
zooming past your ears.
Rocks rub against each other,
Clatter, Rattle, Clack
You grab a pebble,
the roundest one of the bunch.
It sits firmly in the palm of your hand.
The full moon emits a light,
highlighting a path
to the center of the lake.
That is where the stone shall sink.
Your throw was strong,
Pop, Pop, Pop.
It gracefully bounces
obedient to the path.

The water splashes up,
Leaving nothing more than a trail of ripples
And satisfaction to your eyes.

FOR LOVE

by Colleen King

ADELLINE SAT ON a deerskin chair in the middle of her family's wooden cottage, preoccupied with sewing a blanket from fabric patches she had collected over the years. She sat with her feet on another chair beside her while slouching into the warm tan fur behind her. Her little sister bounded down the stairs until she saw Adelline. Then she slowed and walked with perfect posture.

Show off. Mother isn't even here to see you.

Her sister's shadow loomed over, causing Adelline to glance up.

"You really can't act like a proper lady if your life depended on it. It'll do you good later once you're betrothed. Speaking of which, Mother has—"

"Mother has what?" Adelline said. "It's not polite to talk about someone behind their back, Prudence." The creak of old wood redirected the girls' attention to the staircase.

Their mother, old yet perfectly postured, stood at their feet, arms crossed. After a moment of analyzing the siblings, she spoke. "Prudence, go to your room. Adelline, come with me. There are matters to discuss, and it's best if we do so without an audience." She glanced at Prudence. The child bowed her head.

"We're going for a walk." Her mother glanced back at Adelline and then proceeded to the door.

Prudence, as always, followed closely as Adelline and her mother went down the porch's front steps heading towards the quiet little village. A scowl lay across Prudence's face as she hung back on the porch.

Adelline knew her little sister was jealous of her, yet she couldn't tell what there was to be jealous of.

What could Mother want? Adelline pondered, bare feet directing her to the cliffside located by the village. Her anxiety heightened each time her bare foot hit the cool blades of grass, following suit behind her mother's heeled leather boots.

Once they faced the shore below, her mother stopped, hands clasped in front of her body. A hint of longing shone in her grey eyes.

154

Adelline stood a few feet away, her hands connected behind her. "Mother? What was Prudence talking about at home? You must have heard, right?"

The aged woman let out a sigh, gesturing her closer. Adelline didn't budge. "I have betrothed you to a man in the village. His name is Samuel. He's a blacksmith. He's very kind and will make you good m-"

"You've what?" Adelline raised her voice, her body stiffening. She felt her chest tighten. Her skin grew cold at her mother's words. "You expect me to be sold off like a swine to a man I hardly know? Is that why you constantly nagged me to become a proper woman, Mother? Tell me." Adelline yelled over the distant crashing waves and crying seagulls.

"My dear daughter, you should be old enough to understand by now. We aren't a wealthy family. Samuel is a fine man, suited for marriage just as you are. He will bring you good money, and make you happy."

"I don't want money, mother. If I want to marry someone, I want it to be on my own terms, and I would have hoped it would be to someone I had feelings for."

"You think when I was your age I had a choice?" Adelline's mother snapped. Not another word passed between them. Only the sound of waves crashing against the shore broke the thick silence.

Adelline's mind clouded with the looming thought of an engagement, all for money and nothing else. She bolted off to the village and ran towards her family's cottage, where Prudence stood on the front porch and watched as she ran by. Nosy little brat, always trying to curry favor with Mother. Her sister's presence didn't stop Adelline from running into the forest that lay on the outskirts of their village.

Prudence watched her sister disappear and took the last steps down the porch until she stood on the path in front of their cottage. Panic began to set in- she didn't like her sister, but she didn't want her lost, or even worse—dead.

A hand fell onto Prudence's shoulder. "She'll be back. It's only a matter of time before she comes to her senses," her mother said in an unsympathetic tone. She turned to Prudence. "And if not, you'll take her place."

☽ ☩ ☾

Rumors circled the village about this forest. Rumors about men going in to hunt for deer only to never return. Rumors about women falling prey to a creature that lived within its darkness. Rumors about children lured away and never seen again for the rest of their lives. Mutilated bodies of animals found dead on the outskirts, just enough to serve as a warning by whoever- or whatever- lived within its darkness. It was deemed a crime by the village for a person to even go near the edge if they weren't one of the leaders. Yet no one knew for certain what lived within its dark shadows.

But none of that mattered to Adelline. The only thing on her mind was her mother's betrayal. How could she have betrothed her to a man who wouldn't utter a word to her when passing by? Adelline knew her mother only wanted money. Distracted by her thoughts, she slowed from a run to a stiffened walk. She muttered to herself and failed to notice the glowing red eyes that watched her from the shadows.

A shudder ran down Adelline's back. She brought her arms around her torso with hunched shoulders. Her pace slackened as she glanced around and realized where she had gone.

"Well, Mother can't find me now, can she?" She said to herself. "Speaking of—"

She stopped in her tracks, feeling eyes boring into her back. She looked behind and was met with a tall and lean silhouette, a pair of glowing ruby eyes watching her from a few feet away.

"If this is a prank, and you're one of the boys from the village, I'm not interested, nor am I in the mood. In fact, I'm apparently betrothed already. So kindly leave me be." She said, crossing her arms across her chest. The figure did not move or respond. Adelline took a step forward. "I said, *leave me be.*" She spoke louder to the figure. "Are you deaf? Go *away.*" She was yelling now. Her vision blurred with tears, and she attempted to blink them away, before wiping them with the sleeve of her blouse.

An ice cold hand grabbed her chin and lifted it. She saw a handsome young man, his hair the color of a pale daffodil, his eyes glowing a bright rose red. His skin was the color of snow, a beautiful contrast to the darkness of the forest around them. Deep indents lined under his eyes and his cheeks, which appeared deathly sunken in. An old-fashioned suit with a ruffled collar, kept in perfect condition, adorned his figure. Adelline's eyes grew wide.

"Well, now, such a pretty little thing shouldn't wander into the forest alone, should she?" His voice was like a siren's, lulling her smoothly towards death.

The hairs on the back of Adelline's neck stood up in response. She knew better than to fall for it. Her heart began to beat hard. Fight or flight instincts were kicking in as she stared face-to-face with the red-eyed stranger in front of her. Fear crept up on her faster now and grasped her within its icy claws. Yet she stood her ground and never once broke eye contact with him.

"You make a good first impression, don't you?" Adelline said, masking her fear with cockiness.

He grinned in response. Fangs protruded from his upper lip. "Feisty, aren't we? No matter—it makes this more fun."

"This is a game to you, isn't it?" Adelline's eyes narrowed and she brushed his hand from her chin.

"More or less. Now, you said I made a 'good first impression.' I'd like to think I made a *lasting* one." His fangs gleamed as he grinned once again.

At the first twitch from the man, Adelline brought her knee straight into his chest and smacked her palm against his chin. The attack knocked him off his feet.

His back slammed into the ground, and he clutched his head in pain. "I didn't expect that from a small, insignificant mortal…"

Adelline crossed her arms and raised an eyebrow at him. "Are you saying a girl has never put up a fight against you before?"

The man stared at her, astonished. Possibly even impressed. Under his scrutiny, she remained surprisingly calm. Though the thudding of her heart in his eardrums might tell him otherwise.

He chuckled and rubbed his chin with the back of his fingers. "You're a tough one. But, I don't think you were expecting this." His form vanished.

Adelline turned just before he reappeared behind her. "Predictable movement. Look, I know this is all fun and games to you and you're clearly not a human, but I'm not in the mood. I need to clear my head, and I'd appreciate it if you just left me alone to wither in this forest until I grow old, rot, and die. Sounds like a plan?" Adelline stared up at the man.

"You don't fear me?" He paused.

"What?"

"I just noticed—you're speaking as if you have no regards to what happens to your life anymore. Pardon me for asking, but did something happen to you?"

Adelline flinched, but a small smile touched her lips. "You read people well. And you're being oddly *kind*," she noted, gazing into his eyes. "You're staring."

He averted his attention to the side. "Ah, my apologies. I didn't intend to. But really, how did you find yourself here? Your village typically avoids the forest."

Adelline sighed, and explained everything. The arranged marriage, the village, her sister... Everything. He ended up sitting her down on a tree stump while he sat on the grass in front of her. There were moments where she would pause to take in his expression. She finished only after what felt like hours of talking.

The stranger shifted, but a confused look crossed his handsome features. "So this man you're arranged to marry... he does not speak to you?"

"It's not that he can't talk; more like he doesn't want to."

"Perhaps he is shy."

"Samuel? There's no way." Adelline broke out into a fit of laughter. "Samuel is the most cold-hearted person I've ever met. And don't even get me started on his views on marriage. He thinks it's childish. I'm surprised he even accepted my mother's offer..." She gazed off into the dark distance.

The stranger spoke up. "If I may interject, I suspect this is arranged for your mother's personal gain."

"You've just met me and heard my current situation. An hour ago you wanted to kill me. You've never even stepped foot in my village, or met any of my neighbors, or my family. And, if I may point out, we don't even know each other's names. How are you *already* suspicious?"

"Then why not make introductions?"

"I'm sorry?"

"You seem to have a habit of incessant questioning," he said, pointing a finger at her.

Adelline huffed. "Fine. What's your name?" She crossed her legs.

"Claud. Claud Vaughan." He spoke charmingly, and all previous notes of danger vanished from his tone. He sat up on one knee, took her hand in his, and politely kissed Adelline's knuckles.

Her heart fluttered. "Adelline." She said, bowing her head slightly. "It's a pleasure."

"Adelline..." Claud repeated her name. It rolled off his tongue like honey. "Your name means nobility. It's fitting."

"Me, nobility?" She scoffed. "You're kidding. I take back what I said— you don't read people well."

"I meant it in a different sense," he said. "Being noble isn't about being wealthy with fancy clothes and servants at your beck and call. Nobility is having great character. It means being grander than the average. And you *are* grander than the average."

Bold words for someone who attacked me. "How do you know so much about nobility, in the 'fancy clothes' sense, anyway?"

"I'm a noble of sorts, in my world."

"And that would be?"

"Vampires."

Adelline gulped and shuddered at hearing the word out loud.

Claud glanced at her and grinned. "You already could tell though, couldn't you? It's my eyes." He laughed.

Adelline's face went pale.

Claud rubbed the back of his neck. "As I was saying, I come from a prestigious family. A line of purebloods, among the highest ranks of vampires." As he explained, he stood up and paced around her. "My father was a member of Dracula's court. My mother, a lower rank servant in the same court. The Count himself arranged and blessed their marriage. Soon after came the much anticipated birth of me and my siblings. Then—"

"How long ago was that?" Adelline cut in, resting her hands in her lap.

"Over fifty decades ago, Love." He cleared his throat. "We were brought up in a mansion hidden deep in these woods. We were taught skills I'm sure they don't teach in your village."

"Like what?" Adelline raised an eyebrow.

"Fencing, music, ballroom dancing—as well as other skills someone like you couldn't possibly understand," he said. Adelline's eyes narrowed. He looked away from her. "Don't take offense. I'm referring to other skills, like the ones we must develop because we're—"

"Vampires?" She got to her feet and faced the direction she had come. She stroked her hair. "Let me guess, hunting mortals in the night, draining them until they're dry then leaving their corpses for their closest friends and family to see in the morning?"

"More or less," Claud said. His ears perked at the sound of yelling coming from the forest edge, too quiet for Adelline's ears. "Someone is looking for you."

"How do you know?"

"I can hear them. You should leave, before they hunt us both down." He ushered her with his hand on her back towards the way she had come.

"Wait," Adelline stopped and faced him, "if I come back tomorrow, will you find me again?"

"Tomorrow?" Claud's eyes gleamed. He cleared his throat. "Of course. That is, if you do return tomorrow." He smirked.

Adelline turned and walked towards the distant shouting of the village. She could hear a male voice off in the distance. After a few steps, she stopped and glanced at Claud over her shoulder. "You'll have to wait and see." She winked, rushing off into the distant midnight-hued forest.

☽ ✝ ☾

Adelline, completely unharmed, returned to her village just as the sun was beginning to set beyond the horizon. She glanced up only to be met with hickory eyes narrowed at her.

Samuel.

His blacksmith apron was tied around his neck and waist. A hammer sat in his left hand. "Adelline, how did you end up in there? How are you alive?"

"It's none of your concern." Adelline brushed past him. "Interesting that you finally decided to say a word to me."

"It *is* my concern, as your soon-to-be husband. I'm supposed to protect you."

"Don't remind me. Go back to your shop. I'm going to bed."

"How did you end up in that forest in the first place? You know how dangerous it is, especially since we don't know what's in there."

"I said, go *away*, Samuel."

He grabbed her wrist. "Wait."

Adelline flinched and narrowed her eyes at him as Samuel reached into the pocket of his apron. He produced a small, silver band with a dark orange gem perched on top. Adelline's initials were engraved on the inside. Samuel lifted her left palm with his fingertips and slipped the ring onto her finger. "Your mother requested it."

"An engagement ring? Of course she would." Adelline snatched her hand away from his.

"Adelline?"

"What?"

"I'll make you happy. I promise. And I swear, I'm going to protect you from whatever—" His eyes flicked to the forest, then back to her. "Or whoever, is in there."

Adelline froze at his words. Samuel raised an eyebrow. "Sure." She walked off.

Samuel watched her with tense shoulders. As she disappeared from his sight, he stared back towards the forest. Two red, glowing dots caught his

160

attention from the shadows. He only glared back in response. "I know you're in there. And I won't let you take anything away from me."

The dots narrowed then vanished in a flash.

☽ ☩ ☾

After a month of Adelline sneaking off to visit Claud in the forest, she found herself easily falling in love with him- and he returned the feelings to her. One morning, Prudence glanced up from the deerskin chair as her sister danced into the kitchen. Adelline bounded down the stairs with a spring in her step, and hummed a merry tune to herself as she grabbed sweet bread and eggs for breakfast.

She's in a good mood. Prudence watched as her sister swayed to a melody she could not hear.

"Are you hungry, Prudence?" Her sister called to her.

"Sure." Adelline began to double the amount of food she was making. Silence settled through the house.

"Adelline?" Prudence sat up in the chair.

"What?"

"I watched you run into the forest that day. Why do you keep returning?"

Adelline went silent.

"Because ever since you went, you've been acting… different."

"Different?" A giggle escaped Adelline's lips. "Prudence, I'm still me."

"You smiled at me a few days ago."

"Maybe I'm trying to be nicer. You should do the same."

Another silence ensued between the sisters. Prudence took note of the ring on her sister's finger. The gem was no longer dark orange—it had turned blood red.

"Did you meet someone there?"

Adelline's shoulders hunched. "You're ridiculous. No one has ever lived in that forest, and no one ever will."

"If you say so." Prudence gazed at the ring.

"Stop that. Your breakfast is ready. Come eat."

The sisters sat across from each other and ate their breakfast in silence. Adelline was the first to break it. "I'm going out today. Mother asked me to pick up some fabrics and hides from the market while she's visiting her friends."

Prudence tilted her head. "Can I come?"

"Absolutely not. You need to stay inside and watch the house. Understood?"

"Fine." She bit her lip. "Adelline, I know I'm not the best younger sister. But please, don't forget that I love you. I don't want you doing anything stupid… For my and Mother's sakes."

Adelline smiled. "I know." She finished up her breakfast and left her bowl on the table. "I'm going now. I'll see you later."

Adelline could tell from the look on her sister's face she was plotting something. But she brushed the thought away, grabbed her cloak, and headed out the door.

The younger girl followed moments behind her, sneaking around the back of the house until she followed Adelline into the forest. Prudence kept an eye on her sister, all while hiding herself among the dark bushes and trees.

When a dark figure crept up behind Adelline, Prudence nearly screamed, but Adelline didn't tremble. In fact, she was smiling. She turned towards the figure, and Prudence could see it was a pale skinned, cherry-eyed young man. He embraced Adelline with his arms around her waist and placed a kiss on her lips. Prudence stared at them, wide-eyed.

Who is this? Why is he with Adelline?

Prudence slinked away.

I have to tell Mother about this.

A twig caught her foot and sent her face first into the ground. Prudence could hear Adelline gasp and footsteps approach where she lay on the ground.

"It's a child," Claud said, bent over the frightened young girl.

"P-please don't kill me, or my sister," Prudence begged, "We're sorry to trespass, we'll leave, I promise. Please spare us."

He sputtered then burst out into laughter. Adelline approached from behind and gave him a firm elbow in the ribs. He stopped.

"Prudence? What are you doing here?" Adelline bent down to be at her sister's height. The younger girl trembled. Quiet whimpers and pleads came from her trembling lips. Adelline grabbed Prudence's hand.

"You are absolutely, under no circumstances, to ever tell Mother about this. Do you understand me?" She looked into her sister's eyes. Prudence nodded emphatically. "Good. Now go home."

Prudence ran the way she came without a glance back.

☽ ✝ ☾

162

Adelline returned home that night with a red rose in her hands. Her mother was waiting at the door for her.

"Adelline."

Adelline flinched. She saw Prudence hiding behind her mother's skirt. Tears flowed down her cheeks.

"You met a boy? In the forest?" Her mother glowered. "And you've kept him hidden from us? From Samuel? From *me?*" Her voice grated like metal against ceramic. "How did you know he wouldn't kill you? You know the dangers of that place."

Adelline's eyes filled with tears. "You told her. You *told* her." She glared at Prudence. "How could you, Prudence? I thought you loved me.*"

The door to their cottage opened, and Samuel emerged. A silver sword sat in his right hand. A group of men were outside the cottage. Samuel looked past Adelline into the forest. "Restrain her."

One of the men grabbed Adelline's arms from behind. The rose fell from her hands, and was crushed beneath the man's boot as he began attaching shackles to her wrists. She struggled and finally broke free of the grip with a swift kick to the man holding her arms. She bolted off in the direction of the forest.

"After her." Samuel roared, hopping off the porch. He charged in the same direction. Only the man with the shackles followed behind him, while the rest waited anxiously on the outskirts of the village for their return.

☽ ✝ ☾

"Claud!" Adelline called out, already breathless from running. "Claud, please! They're coming. They've found out!"

Like a mist, he appeared in front of her and embraced her while she leapt to bury her face into his chest. All she could do was sniffle while he stroked her hair. The sounds of distant footsteps echoed through the forest. "Come, we need to get you out of here. I'm going to keep you safe, Adelline." He brought his hand to her cheek, and lifted her face up. "We'll be safe, and together. I swear to you."

"I wouldn't be so sure." A husky voice announced. Claud looked up, a low snarl ripped through his throat and chest. It was Samuel, standing behind the couple, sword in his hands.

The other man with the shackles stood behind him. Adelline turned her head, and screamed.

"Adelline, I'm not going to kill you," Samuel said, "but I can do much worse if you don't come with me." He turned to the man behind him. "Grab her. And don't let her escape this time."

"Over my dead body." Claud growled. He shifted his position to protect Adelline behind him. Adeline gripped onto his arms.

"That can be arranged." Samuel grinned. He took notice of his ring on her finger. Where his orange gem once sat, a ruby one now appeared. "Adelline, where is the gemstone in the ring I gave you?"

"I replaced it with my own." Claud stood firm. "She wishes to be with me, and you will respect that."

Samuel's face burned red, and his hand clenched around the base of the silver sword he held. In one motion, he ran forward and struck at Claud. The vampire pushed Adelline aside and dodged the attack.

The man with shackles lunged for Adelline. She ducked out of the way, and he crashed to the ground. A sly grin spread across her face. In response, he lunged again, and Adelline stuck her foot out. He tripped and fell next to her against the dirt of the forest floor. He reached forward, placing one of the metal shackles around her left ankle.

"Claud!" She cried out.

The vampire moved so swiftly, he was a mere blur to Samuel who kept brandishing his sword, only to find Claud had moved behind or in front of him instead.

Then Samuel flashed him a wicked smile. He swung his sword to the side and sliced Claud on his upper arm. The vampire groaned and stumbled back, clutching the spot where Samuel had struck.

"Hurts, doesn't it?" Samuel grinned. "My father was a vampire hunter. He left me his notebook, detailing exactly how to kill a vampire." He raised his sword. "This was one of the swords he used. It's turned thousands of your kind into dust. What say we turn one more?"

Claud closed his eyes. When he reopened them at the sound of a shriek, the wound had healed, his flesh was whole once again.

Sunlight glimmered off the blade in Samuel's hands.

A familiar scent filled Claud's senses.

It was Adelline's. The scent of her blood.

From the tip of Samuel's silver sword crimson red dripped down onto the dirt.

"Claud..." Adelline's voice, once music to his ears, was now nothing more than a strained whisper. She clutched at her heart, blood seeping between her fingers.

Samuel's face froze. He stared at the sword in his hands.

Adelline collapsed, and Claud caught her in his arms. "Hush, my love. You shouldn't talk. You're weak…"

Adelline reached up and placed her hand on his chest.

Claud stroked her neck. "Adelline, I can make you a vampire. I can save your life. Please, let me live longer with you. I know how to do it, I can, just please—"

"No." Adelline's voice was barely audible. "My time is up, Claud."

Tears streamed down his cheeks and fell onto hers. She gave him a weak smile. He placed his own hand over hers.

"I love you," she said. "I only wish we could have spent more time together. Maybe if we went back to that day… Maybe… if you had just killed me…"

"Don't say that," Claud said. "You've changed my life more than you think. I'm never going to meet anyone like you ever again." He took a deep breath, pulling her against him tighter as he exhaled. "I love you. I love you with my whole being. My life is never going to be the same without you…" He broke out into sobs. He placed a final kiss on her forehead then moved to her lips. He could feel her straining to take her final breaths as they parted.

"I'll find you again, one day…" Her hand was cold as it slipped from his cheek. Her ice blue eyes, once so vibrant and care-free, dulled as her life slipped from her and shut closed. Claud wailed as he embraced her against his torso, his face buried deep within her shoulder. He knelt on the ground of the forest.

Samuel, a look of shock and horror on his face, stood motionless. "I only wanted to protect her and keep her safe." He approached the weeping immortal and his dead fiancé's corpse, silver sword still in his hand. "My father once told me about creatures of the night." He stood behind the immortal, the other man with the shackles scurried off towards the village. "How he hunted and killed them by himself, and how I would one day join him to keep our village safe. Until he was killed. By one of your kind."

Claud remained silent.

Samuel leaned over Claud, raising his sword into the air. "I vowed to follow in his footsteps. I vowed to avenge him by killing every one of your kind. I haven't avenged him yet."

As Samuel swung his sword at Claud, the vampire vanished in a flash of blurred movement. Samuel glanced to the side to where Claud laid Adelline's corpse onto a patch of moss and grass with loving tenderness.

"Your blind rage has killed her." Claud, eyes pitch black and fangs exposed, focused on Samuel. "Wasting your life on petty revenge will be your downfall."

Samuel lunged at Claud, his sword aimed at his heart. As the blade was just about to pierce, he froze while Claud vanished once again. A gradual tightening sensation around his throat made him realize exactly where Claud had vanished to.

"Why not join your father, then." Claud growled as he strengthened his grip, squeezing the last breath out of Samuel and throwing his body to the forest ground.

He approached Adelline's corpse, slipped the silver ring off of her finger, and placed it in his palm. He placed a final, tender kiss on her forehead, brushed a strand of hair from her face, and left her there to rest.

"Goodbye, my love."

THE ONE

by Vivien Nguyen

The moon is high in the sky.
It is the midnight of Valentine.
Making sure they aren't dry,
I touch my lips.
The atmosphere surely is sublime.

I finish my plate and
Turn to say my farewells.
He calls out to wait,
And time stops.

Is the feeling right?
Hand on waist, he pulls me closer.
Is it the effects of the night?
Hand on face, he caresses it.
Is the moment right?

Breath reeks of fish
Lips dry as sandpaper.
Face shiny as glass
He comes closer.

I wonder if he is the one.
There are many others out there,
Nothing has truly begun.
Men and women alike,
I would eventually hit the home run.

I push him away.
I throw insults in his ear.
I can't do this, I can't do that.
He's not the one.

WHEN I WAS YOUNG

by Christina Nguyen

When I was young,
My mother would bring me
To a vast field of black lilies.
She would watch me
Frolicking and rolling around
Like a fawn in a new home.

When I was young,
I would see people,
Looking at me with fear
In their eyes
As if I was trying
To be different from them.

When I was young,
I would try to paint
The lucid dreams that haunted me.
The man who repeatedly appeared
With an evil joker's mask and
A smile as hollow and cold
As the shining moon.

When I was young,
Armed with a handful of paintbrushes,
A palette in hand,
And a canvas set out before me,
I fought the nightmares
I painted.

EVENING LIGHT

by Christina Nguyen

The sun's evening rays filtered through the blue window shades.
A warm light fell upon my sleeping face,
As I slowly opened my dazy eyes.

I was sleeping upright, arms folded.
I leaned back against the couch,
Cushions supporting my back.

I remember years ago when a boy confessed to me.
There were some strains between us,
Long breaks with no texts, awkward silences, and more.
I looked back on my high school days,
And wondered how lucky I was to survive.

I found myself crying.
Why?
I clutched a couch pillow tightly,
Thinking about how much things have changed.

ROSE

by Emily Kieu

The day I first met you, you were everything to me.
I always imagined someone sweeping me off my feet.
It seemed like a dream.
Then I remember...
Your dazzling eyes like stars,
Your singing voice when we were in your car.
I always felt a sense of acceptance.
Your scent, like fresh laundry, put me at ease.
I love how you were so patient with me.
You loved me for being me.
Most nights, I miss you.
I miss your genuine smile and your touch.
But am I even enough?
Sometimes, it's hard to sleep.
I toss and turn, wondering,
Where are you?
On days when I'm alone, I still think about you.
Silently, I wonder,
Do you still love me for hurting you?

MY LOVE

by Julie Tran

Although the world may not approve of us, the
Best of me will always belong to you.
Calling you late at night,
Dancing with you until the moon rises,
Eating random food at unpronounceable restaurants,
Falling into your eyes as the hours go by,
Guessing your favorite song,
Hearing your soft and mellow voice,
I can truly say that I love you.
Just for a moment if I could stay, I would
Keep you in my arms for a moment longer.
Looking forward to the future,
Making sure you, my love, believe the world revolves around you.
Not for a moment will you feel unloved,
Oh, that I can do for the rest of my life with no doubt.
Painting the walls of our future house,
Questioning whether it be 5 or 10 years from now.
Reassurance is what I feel,
Staying beside you devotedly.
The way you look at me is out of this world,
Understanding me inside and out,
Varying from my thoughts and slang.
Wishing whatever might be best for me and you,
Xing our souls in this unfair world,
Zip up your jacket, as we go for another round.

My Heart Belongs to the Sea

by Kiwanis Willis

I'm called to the depths
I want to be like water
I want the ebb and flow
The beat of the stones
The rhythm of the waves

The sea foam is a music sheet
The sirens the composers
They sing hymns of sailors
And of those like me
Who are lost at sea

Soup

by Kiwanis Willis

There are so many different types of soup
And just to name a group
There's Bistro, noodle, and chicken
All prepared in a kitchen
Soup makers and soup stores
There are soups galore
If you don't like soup
I'm sorry friend, but you're out of the loop

CHASING GHOSTS

by Colleen King

LAFAYETTE CEMETERY IS WHERE I often find myself on my days off. Most girls my age are out with their friends or boyfriends, getting milkshakes at burger joints and watching cheesy romance films where the two main actors clearly have no bond of any kind.

I'm not like them. I've always been interested in the supernatural, hoping one day to have an encounter with the other world.

I started visiting the burial ground around the same time my best friend moved away to California, and ever since my brother passed away. Since then, I haven't had anyone else to hang out with. It's just too hard to make new friends.

I was walking home alone from spending the entire day at the city's public library when the black metal gate caught my attention. "*Lafayette Cemetery No. 1.*" Its dark gravestones lurking just past the gates drew me in, like a moth to a candle flame. I pushed open the intricately designed gate with ease, a small *creak* making my presence known to the dead. I took a few steps in, and the door clicked close behind me.

What was that? I looked around.

Nothing?

That's too bad.

I walked along the rows of gravestones, moss growing on some, metal ones rusted. The gentle night breeze whispered in the trees. Deeper into the cemetery, I admired the flawlessness of each headstone. A structure loomed in the distance. Odd. I hadn't noticed it before. I carefully stepped around the graves trying to get a closer look.

In front of me stood a large mausoleum carved of gray stone. Its doors opened.

A grin spread across my lips as I crossed the threshold.

Candles inside wall sconces lit up with each step I took. Cold air ran down my back, invigorating me. In the back of the crypt lay a cement casket, surrounded by a layout of candles and candelabras flickering to life as I approached. The smell of wax and burnt wick filled the air.

"What are you doing here?" a voice called out from the darkness.

I froze. "Who's there?"

"I should be the one asking you that," the voice said. A snow white figure emerged, floating up from the stone floor and materializing into a translucent human shape. "After all, you did walk in."

"Who, or what, are you?" I stepped towards the ghostly figure. "Why are you here?"

He looked away, and floated a few steps back.

His cold presence permeated the air. My gaze darted between him and the cement sealed casket behind him.

"What's the matter?" he asked.

"Nothing." I held my hand behind my neck. "I was just admiring the cemetery."

"All by yourself?" He hovered over me, studying my figure. "At this hour?"

"I was just walking home." I shoved my hands into my jacket pockets. "I didn't have anyone else to walk with me anyway, so I took a detour."

"To the cemetery?" His pale eyes traced my figure.

"Yes. I have a certain... passion, I guess you could call it, for the dead. I feel connected to the graves here, if you could believe that." A laugh escaped my lips.

"You're one weird girl..." He muttered under his breath. I pretended like I didn't hear it. "But if you don't mind me asking... Why are you so interested in this?" He gestured around himself.

I opened my mouth to speak, but shut it again. Was I really going to tell a ghost a part of my life that was so personal? *Of course*. When was I going to get another chance like this? Besides... part of him reminded me of William.

"My older brother was killed in a car accident when I was 8 years old. He was 18 when it happened, no more than a year older than I am now. His name was William." I glanced down to my feet as I explained. I heard him take in a breath from above me.

"Not so different from me, huh?" He chuckled, and for a moment, I could see his eyes flash with a distant pain I couldn't understand. Not yet, anyway.

Over the course of a few weeks, every time I've walked into the mausoleum where we first met, he's been there. As docile as he's proven to be, he still never fails to cause my heart to race and my mind to run wild with curiosity. However, these feelings vanish as soon as my eyes discern his figure, resting peacefully atop the marble coffin, his eyes often closed, yet on occasion fluttering open. He's never really asleep—I know better. I know he can't.

"You've found me," he whispered, his voice settling in the air.

"Of course," I said, my hands clasped behind my back. "You aren't very good at hiding yourself, you know." I pointed out to him with a sly grin adorning my face.

He responded with a chuckle. "I wasn't trying to, this time. I was, however, trying to take a—what do people call it again—a nap?"

He sat up and faced me, his transparent, snow white skin glowing in the dim moonlight that shone through the colorful stained glass windows of the empty crypt.

"You and I both know you can't sleep," I said.

He shrugged and went back to lying on his back with his eyes closed once again.

"Adam." I groaned, trudging over to his deathly still position on the coffin. I noticed an engraved faded gold plaque at the foot of it. How had I never noticed it before? This grave was actually occupied. "Hey, that's disrespectful."

"What? My ignoring you because I want to 'nap' isn't disre—"

"No. You're lying on a dead person."

I attempted to shove him off of the marble encasing, the thought of there being a deceased person's remains just beneath its cover. My hands went right through his chest. Adam didn't notice, didn't even budge. How could he just treat this as something trivial?

The more I made a scene of trying some way to get him off, the less he moved from his position. I gave up with a loud groan.

"How can a ghost be so stubborn?"

"How can a mortal be so concerned over a long-dead stranger? My life ended so long ago, and so abruptly, you shouldn't even be concerned in the first place." he said in a deepened voice.

I stepped away from him. I felt my fingers twitch and my heart beat faster. I guess ghosts really have no concern for the resting dead. I understood why, they have nothing to lose, but to witness it from someone I've come to consider a close friend… It hurt. A tightening in my chest forced me to speak up to him.

"How dare you."

"Excuse me?"

175

"Adam, how dare you," I said, throwing my hands up in disbelief. "You're lying on top of someone. Someone who had a family, friends, a *life*. And you're treating it like it's a *bed? You can't even sleep.*"

"I had a family. I had friends. I had a life too. Yet someone stripped it away from me, in the blink of an eye."

I stopped. "Adam? How did you die?"

"Wouldn't you like to know? Since you're so obsessed with the dead, ever since your dear older brother Will died, huh?"

"Don't even *start* with that, Adam."

"And why shouldn't I? You want to know how I died so badly? Fine. I was killed. Stabbed in the back by a woman who I thought I would spend the rest of my life with. I was betrayed, and left for dead after she took everything away from me. Happy now?"

"Adam... I didn't mean to..."

My voice seemed to reach deafened ears.

He paused, opened one pale eye, and turned his head to face me before opening the other. "I forgot to let you read the plaque."

I clutched a hand to my chest, and stomped over to the foot of the marble coffin again. The name engraved into the rusted gold caused me to hold my breath.

❖ *Adam Belizaire* ❖
Born 1845, Deceased 1863, Died at 18 years of age.

I let out a shaky breath and realized how tightly my own hand was clutching onto the collar of my shirt. Adam was sitting up now, staring down at me. The air around both of us had relaxed, for the moment.

"Keep reading."

I returned my eyes to the plaque.

A beloved son and a friend to all. May his soul rest in Heaven with God as he watches over us from above.

I stood, frozen in place. I began to imagine how his funeral had gone about. Was he truly loved by everyone? Was he as naturally flirty and open back then? Questions buzzed in my mind.

Adam never even talked about his human life. He only told me that he was a spirit and couldn't cross over into Heaven nor Hell, who was stuck roaming the earth, taking on a mere mirage of his living self. That was all.

My gaze rose from the plaque to his ghostly figure. He was on his knees, his hands rested on his thighs.

"Well?" The features of his face relaxed, yet his eyes were alert, and bright.

"Adam, I had no clue. I'm so sorry. I thought you only chose to meet here because it was out of anyone's view..." I spoke in a quiet voice, averting my gaze from his. I felt a soft breeze wrap under my chin and tilt it up. My eyes met his.

"What are you apologizing for?" he said. I realized the fog I felt was his hand raising my chin up.

I heaved out a sigh. "I just—I was just too fascinated by what you were to even realize that this is *your* grave. *Your* body is inside of here, mere bones and maybe bits of-"

"All right, enough of that. I don't want to envision my own handsomeness rotting in a wooden box." He chuckled. I couldn't help curl my lips into a smile, but his expression became stoic again. "... Do you want to know more?"

"If you don't mind."

"Alright then. When I was sixteen years old, I fell in love with a girl the same age as me. Her name was Maria. She was beautiful, and everything I wanted. But I didn't know she had other plans. You see, my family was one of the wealthiest in our town. My father was a plantation owner, and that's all that mattered to the girls in my town, apparently. I thought Maria was different. When both of us turned eighteen, we discussed a plan to run away and get married, to avoid the lives our parents had planned out for us. She told me to pack enough money and supplies for at least a week's trip, and I did. We planned to meet one summer night, out in my father's fields, where we would run away into the night. As it turns out, she had planned with a secret lover to kill me and steal my fortune. As I waited for her, he stabbed me from behind and she took everything, right in front of my dying eyes. I didn't wake up until the next morning, where I saw my bloodied body lying in the fields with my family, and the workers, standing over me."

"Adam... Oh my gosh... I'm so sorry."

"I'm dead, Liz. There is nothing to apologize for. If I didn't want you visiting my grave, I wouldn't have opened my mausoleum for you in the first place. But I believe I'm still stuck here, longing for a reason to move on… I just haven't found it yet."

"Adam."

He laughed in response. "The point is, I was lonely. I felt the energy you were giving off—you were lonely as well. I was interested, and I opened the doors. You're the one that snuck in here."

I pouted at him.

There was silence between us, and for a moment I could feel the air beside him getting warmer. His eyes looked beyond my shoulder to the stained glass windows. They were beginning to glow with the gentle lumination of moonlight.

"It's getting late, my dear—you should go back home," he said. "It's been a long night."

"But, Adam, I still have more questions."

"I'll be sure to answer them soon. So long as you come visit me." His gentle smile returned to his features, but the same distant pain from the first time we met gleamed in his eyes once again.

I nodded. "Tomorrow night it is, then. Be prepared with answers—I might end up writing a book about this one day."

"I'll be looking forward to it."

Just as I was out the door, Adam called out to me.

"And do *try* to make *living* friends soon," he said with a smirk.

The following night, I stepped into the graveyard ready with a small leather-bound notebook and a pen tucked underneath my arm. I stepped over each grave carefully, and maneuvered my way over to the mausoleum as I always had done for the past weeks with Adam. Before I stepped through the door, I took a deep breath, and prepared for what I was about to hear. I couldn't believe it—after looking for answers from the other side for so long, I was finally going to be able to hear them firsthand. I pulled out the notebook from underneath my arm, and stepped inside.

Inside the large mausoleum was unsettlingly quiet. The candles lining the walls didn't light up when I passed. The air was cold, seeming to be frozen in time with the chilly cold air of the night.

"Adam? You're going to be shocked when I tell you what happened at school today. I actually think I made a *living friend*. Are you shocked?" My voice echoed off of the cement walls. There was no response.

"... Adam?" I called out again. Still no reply.

"Come on, Adam. If you're hiding, this isn't funny. You know what happened last time you tried to jump out and scare me; I'm immune to that stuff, remember?" No voice replied, and no ghostly figure appeared before my eyes as I scanned the entire mausoleum. I checked behind the cement casket, peaked through the stained glass window—nothing. I set my notebook and pen on the lid, and trailed my gaze around the perfectly preserved grave one more time. My eyes eventually hit the plaque once again, and I couldn't help but read it over.

It finally hit me. He wasn't here anymore. He had finally moved on.

And so had I.

OH, THE AUDACITY

by Kimbill Ly

Audacious fools
Bringing courage whilst in fits of hubris
Collect, often in graves
Don't dig up that forbidden valor
Enough is enough, bury it deep
Forget about that strength and let it sleep
Gratuitous bursts of bravery
Have no place in this rotten sanctuary
Isles of tombs line down the cemetery
Justly so, as it was the Lord's order
Killed for conveying too much will
Locked within caskets for chasing thrills
Mortuaries filled as a result of audacity
Never worth it, never fair
Omens from the gods
Peaceful times, they sought
Quietness, they fought
Rampaging wails, they brought
Sorrowful times
Thrown were their lives
Ultimately sacrificed
Valiantly placed down
Walking towards the light
Xanthan and moss cover the ground
Youthful legacies lost, and
Zealots would ask, at what cost?

SILENCE

by Kimbill Ly

I sit in solemn silence in a dull, dark room
Hands to the paper as if they were sweeping brooms
The silence is unbearable,
The silence is chaotic,
The silence is too loud
I get up and push the door open
exit the room and walk outside,
Exposing myself to the disorder and chaos surrounding my home,
There is nothing but commotion,
Sweet cozy commotion
The volume is welcome,
The volume is tranquil,
The volume is so pleasant
All I can hear now is peace

CHRONIC ILLNESS

by Darby Vaughn

Awkward and dissociating.
Those are the first two words I could think of for my chronic illness.

To me, my illness is that one awkward kid,
Who was invited by a friend of the acquaintance to the cousin of the
host of a party,
Who doesn't really enjoy or partake in the celebration of a person or
thing,
But who enjoys the picture and aesthetic of being the quiet kid,
Who's glued to the corner of the room or to the friend who invited
them.
Who enjoys the pretty colors and the mind-numbing music surrounding
them.
Who enjoys looking at their surroundings, but not being a part of it.

To me, my illness is a dissociating thought.
It's the out-of-body experience you get in the middle of class or during a
lecture,
When your mind begins to wander and you're a little too tired to keep
your head on straight.
It's the blaringly peaceful feeling of hollowness that you typically feel,
When you know that you should be focusing on something else entirely,
But all you can think of is how you, yourself, feel like a moving picture,
That's simply stuck in a first-person perspective.
It's the feeling of heavy weightlessness,
That you both longed and dreaded feeling again.
With your head empty of thought,
And your stomach churning with unease.

Years in the future, maybe someone will read this and ask,
"What did the author mean when she said…"
And I'll be honest that I wouldn't know either,
Because that's what chronic illness really is.
It's a cohesive word and a messy sentence.
It's both an experience and a lifestyle.
It's both a part of an identity and also not.

To you, it is a threat that I could drop dead at any moment,
But for me, it's just another day of counting down carbs and stressing
over insulin.
But maybe that's why people without this illness see it as something
interesting,
Something unique and new,
Why people will ask you uncomfortable questions and treat you
differently.
Not because they are trying to be rude or invade of your privacy,
But simply because they want to know more.
They want to understand it beyond the stereotypes and beyond the
media coverage.
Or maybe that's just what I like to think.

MISTAKE

by Vy Ngo

It's easy to forget that humans
Are indeed humans.
Like a broken treadmill, we keep running.
We trip and fall, injure our hearts,
But we keep running
Until the treadmill truly dies.
If we allow ourselves to trip
Then our thoughts would not spiral
Like endless turtles stacked at the bottom of the Earth.
It's easy to forget
That mistakes are like sandpaper.
We use them to scrub away our past,
But scrub too much, we damage ourselves.
Unlike a turtle,
Our mistakes don't last.
They go away, no matter how hard we cling to them.
So let go like a waterfall,
Let your mistakes fall, but don't fall with them.
Remember the bottom of the mountain.
That's where your mistakes go.
So learn, and let go.

OLD MAN

by Vy Ngo

Tell me, Old Man,
Where do I stand
At the end of the road?
Tell me, Old Man,
What am I to you?
The road seems endless
But you always hold my hand
Tell me, Old Man,
What am I to do?
Will you be here when I get there?
"One foot at a time," you say.
Tell me, Old Man,
Where will you be?
Will you see how far I've come?
This road I'm on is lonely, you know.
But I feel your hand,
Gently pushing against my back
The force compels me
"You'll be okay," you say.
I feel your hand,
Grasping my shoulder,
But you don't pull me back.
Tell me, Old Man,
Will you be with me forever?
"No," you say. "But I'll be here."
Old Man, you disappear,
But you'll always be here.

I'm Not Lost, I'm Still Finding Myself

by Ann Quach

You find yourself again—in bits and pieces—
The gaping holes patched up with wild lines of thick glue
and careful, careful rows of surgical stitches.

There are fragments found—
at 3:00 in the morning, in the drive-through of a McDonalds
while ordering large fries and a black coffee,
or in the way the light reflects and the shadows dance
on your car window at 1:00 in the afternoon,
or in the deep blue of a cold ocean, steady waves at your feet.
You find yourself again—
in bright colors and loud laughs and favorite songs.

And maybe you lose parts, too—
carefully hoarded scraps seem to slip from your hands all over again,
dropped and forgotten in dark corners and dirty bathrooms.
It's terrifying—to feel as if you'll never be whole again
But humans are works in progress—incomplete by nature—
filled with holes and bruises and scars.
So maybe you have some holes that don't quite close
and scars that still ache—
maybe those parts are meant to be lost
maybe—maybe you come off stronger for it.

You find yourself again—
It takes weeks, months, years
of thorough planning and crass patchwork,
but slowly, without notice, it creeps up on you

You'll be brushing your teeth, glancing at the mirror—
and loving what you see.

You'll find that you haven't just survived—
you'll find that you've *lived*.

—I'm not lost, I'm still finding myself

SCULPTURE

by Kenneth Tran

the girl took delicate steps
toward the azure waters that surrounded her world
her white jade skin unsullied, untouched
her eyes reminiscent of an arctic pearl

her blonde hair contrasted the coral sky
swaying in the breeze
uncoordinated, but graceful
a truly exquisite duality

her feet became embraced by a gentle rush
the fair blue color swirled
against her leg, she was a part of it
a cerulean sculpture with the world

it retreated, revealing a shimmering caramel brown
that found its way into her hand
blazing, beaming, brilliant
a violet shell appeared within the sand

AUTHOR BIOS

Diane Bui

Originally from Fountain Valley, California, Diane Bui has grown up with an affinity to the arts such as drawing, music, and writing. She continues to seek her purpose in life while respecting the purpose of others. Along the way, she finds time to enjoy good food and kind friends.

Vi Bui

Having grown up in Westminster, Vi Bui discovered a passion for art and writing which fueled her spark for life. She specializes in romance and comedy genres and hopes to pursue a career in writing.

Cattu Do

Born in California, raised in Garden Grove, passionate about poetry—this describes Cattu Do. As a child, she expressed her feelings through poems and fell in love with the written art. She plans to continue writing poetry, perhaps completing a poetry book of her own.

Julia Do

Julia Do, from Westminster, California, serves as copy editor of Del Sol. Recognized by the Scholastic Art and Writing Awards, she attended the Kenyon Review Young Writers Workshop in 2019, and her oil paintings and poetry have appeared in Canvas Literary Journal and Blue Marble Review.

Mariana Escalona Diaz

Born in Mexico and moving all the way from San Juan Capistrano, California, up to Glendale, and back down to Orange County, Mariana Escalona Diaz has had the opportunity to connect with different cultures. Growing up, it was difficult for her to express her emotions until she discovered poetry, and her voice.

Keanu Hua

An author inseparable from the multicultural experience, Keanu Hua writes with the impulsive collision of a spoiled childhood and the morbid tastes of today, writing that ponders the other shores of life – ones that were not as fortunate as his own – and how these peculiar paths leave long-lasting legacies.

An Huynh

An Huynh was born and raised in California with a love for books, poetry, and music. She is often inspired by songs and hopes to write a song of her own in the future. She has goals of writing more and becoming a journalist.

Marcello Juarez

Born in California, Marcello Juarez grew up in Santa Ana where he developed a great sense of creativity and imagination. Despite being a story writer since the fourth grade, "The Night Sky" is his first published poem. One day, Marcello wants to fulfill his dream of becoming a game developer.

Emily Kieu

An Asian-American California-based girl, Emily Kieu lives life through the moments she shares with her friends and family. While she used to focus her time on Wattpad, she now devotes her energy towards league and writing stories.

Colleen King

Born in Fountain Valley, Colleen King is the youngest with three older brothers, including the infamous author, Zachary King. When she's not huddled in the corner writing supernatural stories, she's in her dance studio with her pointe shoes on doing ballet, or drawing in one of her many, many sketchbooks.

Michelle Lam

Michelle Lam is a high school sophomore from Westminster, California who loves to write and draw. Although she doubts her survival to adulthood, she dreams of being an author of a novel one day. When she's not writing, she hangs out with her sister, constantly waiting for summer.

Bryce Le

Born in Southern California, Bryce Le was raised in Westminster, where they developed an interest in writing, breathing, and being a general nuisance to those around them. They aspire to be an engineer someday in the future, but would be satisfied with just getting a job at all.

Shannon Le

From Southern California, Shannon Le is an art lover, a music geek, and a fan of fantasy books. Her stories and poems are where she expresses her imagination and observations of life. In the future, Shannon hopes to see the Seven Wonders of the World.

Brian Ly

From the Lands of Oz, Brian Ly found himself spending much of his life in California. Though he was not always a writer, Brian's recent interest in Dungeons and Dragons has led him to pick up a pen and paper. On an unrelated note, he strives for a career in mathematics.

Kimbill Ly

Born and raised in California, Kimbill Ly discovered his passion for literature as soon as he began his education at the age of five. He has a profound interest in writing about human morals, or lack thereof, and philosophy.

Vy Ngo

Vy Ngo was born in Vietnam and immigrated to the United States in 2011. She loves writing plays, studying history and reading books. She hopes to become a teacher and inspire future generations of students.

Christina Nguyen

Aloof and mostly reserved, Christina Nguyen has a love-hate relationship with sleep and a love for boba and music. Fighting her forever growing senioritis and writer's block, Christina enjoys writing stories when she's not teasing her younger brother. Currently, she can be found daydreaming with her panda plushie.

Kayla Nguyen

Growing up, Kayla was surrounded by innovation and creativity. She developed an interest in the arts as well as in the different fields of science. Kayla has been drawing and writing since second grade, and hopes to become an astronomer one day.

Michelle Nguyen

Michelle Nguyen grew up in Westminster, California where she developed her interest in music and writing. She loves to express her thoughts through writing poems and hopes to pursue a career in neuropsychology in the future.

Terry Nguyen

Born in Fountain Valley, Terry Nguyen has lived in Westminster his whole life. Surrounded by technology from a young age, he quickly got into the internet, particularly the games that came with it. Terry hopes one day to pursue a career in law enforcement.

Vivien Nguyen

Vivien Nguyen grew up with an appreciation for the arts. She enjoyed creating illustrations, both digitally and traditionally. In middle school, her love for the arts blossomed. Taking all the art courses she can, she continues to develop her skills in hopes of one day becoming an art director.

Katherine Pham

Raised in Anaheim, Katherine Pham has been in love her entire life with all forms of art, the essence of her spirit. On weekends, she can be found longboarding with friends, coding an RPG game, playing League of Legends, or doing community service.

Ann Quach

Growing up in Orange County as a Vietnamese-American, Ann Quach finds poetic inspiration from her family, culture, and society. Her first published poem, "I am a second-generation immigrant," details the struggles her family faced while searching for a better life in a new country.

Andrea Torres

Andrea Torres, born and raised in Garden Grove. She enjoys watching clouds move across the sky and is constantly thinking of new ideas, seeking inspiration. In the future, Andrea hopes to earn her degree in Human Service so that she can help others on their path to success.

Julie Tran

Originally from Ho Chi Minh of Vietnam, Julie Tran moved to the city of Westminster when she was around three years old. As the years passed and she grew up, she developed a love for swimming, music, and cooking. One day, Julie hopes to be a successful writer.

Kady Tran

Born and raised in California, Kady Tran discovered how to bring her imagination onto paper and weave it into love stories. Her passion for writing came from countless Wattpad stories she read, including best-selling romance novels. When not reading romances, she is watching them in movies and shows.

Kenneth Tran

Kenneth Tran was born in Fountain Valley where he lived a very simple childhood. His young fascination with reading formed an eagerness to express his wild imagination onto art and paper. He wishes to be in a profession where he gets to use his creativity.

Benson Truong

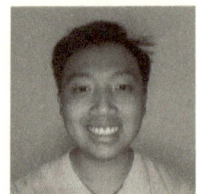

Originally from Southern California, Benson Truong grew to become a funny, dependable, and genuine. An amateur artist, he devotes time to creating realistic drawings and portraits. Recently, he's been exploring photography and cinematography with the goal of capturing moments in life he never wants to forget.

Darby Vaughn

Darby Vaughn was born in Orange County, California and currently resides in Santa Ana. As she's grown up she has picked up an interest in everything that relates to art, from drawing to writing. Although she has written countless personal poems, this is her first publication.

Christine Vu

Back for her second year in Creative Writing, Christine Vu stepped out of her comfort zone to join the editing team. Other than writing, she enjoys image editing and listening to European music. She looks forward to a future working behind-the-scenes in the film industry.

Kathleen Vu

Born and raised in California, Kathleen has been writing poems since third grade. She likes punk rock music, dogs, and science. Kathleen identifies under the asexual/ aromantic spectrum, which is reflected in her first published work. She supports mental health awareness, and hopes to become a doctor.

Kiwanis Willis

Kiwanis Willis is a cat and manga enthusiast who grew up in Garden Grove. He spends his free time playing video games and watching movies. The only thing wilder than his hair is his insatiable love for ramen.

Alexa Wright

A curious student from California, Alexa Wright has spent hundreds of hours building contraptions, writing code, and sifting through piles of papers to catch addition errors. As she leaves her childhood behind, she hopes to use writing to express the ideas, dreams, and fears of her formative years.